'Can I come in

Tina's heart turned
welcome.

'I know it's late, and I'm sorry about that. I just wanted to apologise again about tonight. I take it Josh is in bed?'

'And, for once, asleep,' she confirmed.

Her face set and he sighed inwardly, guessing what the problem was. 'Tina, I'm not trying to push you. I'm not trying to take Rod's place and muscle in on Josh.'

'Aren't you?'

'No. I...' He raked a hand through his hair. 'I'm not used to saying things like this and it's bound to come out wrong. I like you. No. I more than like you. You blow my mind. But I know you're not over Rod and you've got Josh to think of. So I'd like to be friends with you.'

'*Just* friends?'

'If it turns into something else, that's fine by me. I'm happy to wait until you're ready.'

Kate Hardy lives on the outskirts of Norwich with her husband, two small children, two lazy spaniels—and too many books to count! She wrote her first book at age six, when her parents gave her a typewriter for her birthday. She had the first of a series of sexy romances published at age twenty-five, and swapped a job in marketing communications for freelance health journalism when her son was born so she could spend more time with him. She's wanted to write for Mills & Boon® since she was twelve—and when she was pregnant with her daughter, her husband pointed out that writing Medical Romances™ would be the perfect way to combine her interest in health issues with her love of good stories. It really is the best of both worlds—especially as she gets to meet a new gorgeous hero every time…

Recent titles by the same author:

A BABY OF HER OWN
HIS EMERGENCY FIANCÉE

HER SPECIAL CHILD

BY
KATE HARDY

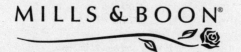

For CGRB. Because ADHD children are very, very special.

*First published in Great Britain 2003
Harlequin Mills & Boon Limited,
Eton House, 18-24 Paradise Road, Richmond, Surrey TW9 1SR*

© Kate Hardy 2003

ISBN 0 263 83458 1

*Set in Times Roman 10½ on 12 pt.
03-0703-47973*

*Printed and bound in Spain
by Litografia Rosés, S.A., Barcelona*

CHAPTER ONE

'COME in!'

Alex opened the door to the locum's room, ready to give his welcoming speech, and his chin virtually hit the floor.

Purple hair. She had *purple hair*!

That aside, she was stunning. Huge violet-blue eyes in a heart-shaped face that just begged to be cupped between his hands, a smile that made the base of his spine tingle, a mouth that promised sensuality and made him want to lower his own to it and kiss her until—

Oh, great. Just what he needed. A goddess in the spare consulting room. Why couldn't she have been middle-aged, the sort who was like everyone's favourite aunt? But no. Maggie, his practice manager, had landed him with the most gorgeous woman he'd ever seen. The sort who could easily tempt him away from his vow of celibacy, even first thing on a Monday morning when his mind was focused completely on work.

Except for one fact. He'd seen her hopping up the hill towards the local primary school twenty minutes earlier with an equally purple-haired small child, so she was obviously married—that made her very firmly off limits. Unlike Vivi, he respected marriage vows.

She smiled again and his heart stopped.

This really, really wasn't fair.

'You must be Alex Bowen. I'm Tina Lawson, the locum,' she said, standing up and holding out her hand. 'Welcome back.'

He shook her hand, noting the firmness of her grip. It was reassuring and professional and very doctor-like—but the touch of her skin also did something else to him. Every nerve-end that touched her was tingling. Worse, he could clearly imagine what other parts of her skin would feel like against his fingertips, soft and warm and smooth and tempting. What she'd feel like beneath his mouth, how she'd taste...

Stop it, his common sense commanded. *She's a colleague. Be professional.*

But the words that came out weren't exactly professional. 'You're not what I expected.'

She chuckled as she released his hand. 'The hair, you mean?' She gestured to her bright purple fringe as she sat down again. 'I guess I've overdone it just a tad.'

Beautiful, clever *and* funny. Resisting her was going to be like the seven labours of Hercules, multiplied a thousandfold.

Tough. You have to. So meet lightness with lightness, he told himself. 'Just cross your fingers that you don't get certain people on your list this morning.'

'Or I'll be in for a lecture, you mean?' She grinned back. 'Nah. The younger ones will love it—and the older ones have known me so long they'll either tease me about it or mutter darkly that they always knew young Tina'd come to a bad end.'

Eh? She wasn't local, surely? He'd lived in Ellingthorpe for nearly six years now and he'd never met her. And Tina Lawson, even without the purple hair, wasn't someone he'd forget in a hurry.

She rattled a collecting tin at him. 'Anyone who comments about my hair can give some money to school funds. Starting with you.'

He gave in with good grace and emptied the change

from his pockets into her tin. 'The school talked you into this, did they?'

'Not exactly. The children each paid a pound to be out of uniform and have mad hair for a day. It's a fundraiser for some sports equipment. Josh decided he wanted his hair purple, so we sprayed it this morning, and then he started panicking that people would laugh at him. So I kept him company.' She gestured to her fringe again. 'It'll wash out. Tomorrow morning, I'll be back to sober Dr Lawson, but today I'm doing this for my little boy. It's important to him. I'm sure the patients will understand.'

Putting her child before her job. Again, Alex felt that weird clenching in his stomach and pushed the thought away. He knew not everyone was like Amanda, who had always put her job first and rushed family time so she could get back to whatever important research she'd been doing. Or like Vivienne, who—

Stop right there. It was nobody's fault. Not Vivi's, not yours. Remember where you are. Work.

But he still couldn't concentrate. The way she'd said 'my little boy', her face filled with love and pride, had knocked his composure for six. He couldn't help glancing at her left hand.

No ring. No tell-tale pale band of skin to report a recently removed ring either. Divorced, or never married? And where was Josh's father? Was he still around, or...?

None of your business, he reminded himself.

'The colour of my hair doesn't affect the way I do my job,' she added, a shade defensively this time.

'Of course not. Have you settled in OK?' Daft question. Of course she had. She was local, wasn't she? And what was he going to do next—leer at her and ask her if he could, ahem, help her settle in a little better, young lady? Oh, puh-*leese*. He had to work with the woman for the next couple of weeks. The only relationship they could possibly have was a working one. End of story. Even if she wasn't married with kids, she was a colleague and that made her off limits.

Though a tiny imp was sitting just above his left ear, whispering suggestions. *Supposing she isn't married? No ring, remember. And she's only a temporary colleague. Ask her out to lunch.*

No. I've already been there, done that and picked up the smithereens afterwards, shard by painful shard.

She's different.

That's not the point.

She's gorgeous.

Also not the point.

But wouldn't you like to…?

Whoa. Stop right there.

Because, yes, he would like to. Very much. Alex surreptitiously raked his fingers through his hair and flicked the imp off his perch. Then he concentrated on what Tina was saying.

'It's been great. Maggie filled me in on all the admin side of things, and Adam, Mark, Sharon and Julie make a good team,' she said, referring to the other three partners and the practice nurse. 'We've kept up the Wednesday morning meetings while you've been away.'

She seemed perfectly at home here. As if she'd been here for ever, rather than three short months. 'Thanks for stepping in at such short notice.' Very short notice: it had only been two days before the previous locum had been scheduled to start, when he'd broken his leg on a weekend climbing trip. Which was why Alex hadn't met Tina Lawson—he'd been in Liverpool at the time, so Maggie had had to sort out a replacement.

'No problem. Um—I was sorry to hear about your mother,' she said.

'Thank you.' It had been a rough three months, watching Amanda fade slowly—and even then there had still been a reserve between them. She'd still tried to convince him to leave general practice and follow in her footsteps, and he'd still been longing to hear her say the words he couldn't remember from his childhood.

They'd both been disappointed.

'I've enjoyed working here. I'll be sad to leave,' Tina said.

Leave. That reminded him about the brief phone conversation he'd had with Maggie the previous night when he'd still been too bone-weary to take things in, but what his practice manager had said returned to him now with a snap. With the new development on the edge of the village, their practice had expanded to the point where they needed another partner. But finding one could take months. They needed help, and they needed it now. He had to make a decision. Fast. 'You're with us for another fortnight, aren't you?'

She nodded.

'If you don't have anything else lined up, we'd like you to stay for a bit longer.' Although he had his reservations—the purple hair aside, what she did to his composure and the way she encouraged the imp was extremely worrying—Maggie had said Dr Lawson was good with the patients. 'Say, three months?' Which would give them a breathing space to advertise and interview applicants.

Her eyes widened. 'Really?'

At his curt nod, that beautiful mouth curved into another smile, a smile that gave him a weird sensation between his ribs. A heart-turning, nerve-end-prickling sensation. A sensation that made him want to…

Go on, Alex, the imp said, having climbed back onto his perch. *Forget protocol, forget work, forget everything—just sweep her up in your arms and ride off into the sunset.*

He managed to control himself and the imp. Just. 'I'll let you get on with surgery. Catch you later.' The last bit was completely insincere. He was staying well away from Tina Lawson—unless he had a very long, very cold shower first.

Tina leaned back in her chair as Alex left the room and took a deep breath, then slowly exhaled again. Why hadn't Maggie warned her? Why hadn't Maggie *told* her that the senior partner was drop-dead gorgeous? Tall, dark and sexy—he had to have an Italian ancestor somewhere, with his beautiful almost-black eyes and the dark hair that fell forward over his eyes. Mr Darcy. No, not quite right, though she had to suppress the thought of Alex Bowen in old-fashioned riding gear, with a wet, ruffled white shirt clinging to his skin. Not Mr Darcy. More brooding than that: Heathcliff. With a sensual mouth like that, he was born to play Heathcliff, passionate and elemental and—

She flinched. Even now, she still saw people in terms of parts they were born to play. A game she and Rod had started all those years ago, to while away the time waiting for his auditions and give her a break from her studies. She'd always gone to auditions with him, when she hadn't been in lectures. He'd said she brought him luck.

And the one audition where she hadn't gone with him...

She shivered and pulled herself together. Not here, not now. She had a job to do. She pressed her buzzer to let Lorraine, the receptionist, know she was ready for her first patient.

'How are you today, Mrs Martin?' she asked as the elderly woman slowly made her way to the chair and sat down.

'Not so bad. Just a bit stiff.' The old lady gave her an arch look. 'Not sure that colour's really you, though, young Tina.'

'The hair, you mean? Yes, it's a bit bright. It's for Josh's school fundraiser,' Tina explained with a rueful grimace.

Mrs Martin glanced at the tin, then struggled to open her handbag.

'You really don't need to—' Tina began.

'Tina Lawson, I've known you since you were knee-high to a grasshopper. If you're doing something for a good cause, it's worth giving money for,' was the tart reply.

'Then thank you,' Tina said as the old lady put some change in the tin. She barely needed to glance at her notes. 'So the consultant's confirmed what I thought—that it's the early stages of Parkinson's?'

'Yes. But I don't see how. You know old Len down the road—well, he had Parkinson's and he used to shake like a good 'un.'

'Not everyone gets all the symptoms,' Tina said.

'I was so sure it was arthritis.' Mrs Martin shook her head. 'Runs in the family, it does—my old mum had it bad. I thought that's what all the aches and pains were in my legs, my hips.'

'Though you didn't have the swelling that normally goes with arthritis,' Tina pointed out gently, 'and then there were the other things—tiredness, needing to get up to the loo four or five times a night, your voice going quieter.'

Plus the slight shuffling movements Mrs Martin made,

her torso stooped slightly forward and her arms not swinging the way they usually did when she walked, the difficulty in getting out of a low chair, the slight depression, the constipation that the old lady had been too embarrassed to admit to until Tina had gently asked if she needed some help. Which was why Tina had referred her for an X-ray to confirm there weren't any bone deformities, to rule out any suspicion of osteoarthritis, then to a neurologist.

'It's more common than you'd think.' It affected around one in a hundred people aged sixty to seventy—Mrs Martin's age group—men and women alike. 'It starts off so mildly that you've probably had it for years. Though it's not hereditary—we don't actually know what causes it. Has the appointment with the Parkinson's nurse come through yet?'

'Next Wednesday,' the old lady confirmed.

'Good. She'll be able to give you some practical tips about coping, and information about help they can give you with special furniture, handrails and equipment to make life easier for you. In the meantime, we'll start you on the drugs—we'll change the dose every week for the next eight weeks, until we find the one that suits you best. They should help a lot with the pain, and you'll find it easier to move. I think you'll start seeing a difference by the end of next week. And then, when we find the dose that makes you feel back on top of the world, we'll carry on with that one.'

Mrs Martin nodded. 'Thank you.'

'The Parkinson's nurse should be able to answer most of your questions, but if you're worried about anything at all, just come and see me. I want to see you every two weeks for the next eight weeks anyway, so we can review your treatment and see how you're feeling,' Tina added.

'Rightio.'

Tina printed out the prescription and signed it, then handed it to Mrs Martin with several sheets of paper. 'Your family's bound to want to know more, and sometimes it's difficult to remember what anyone's said, so this is just some information about Parkinson's.' Information she'd produced, the previous week, for the surgery website. The website Maggie had agreed to in Alex's absence…

The others had all been happy about it, and she was writing the content in the evenings, while Josh was asleep. It wasn't taking up any time from her surgery hours, and it was helping the patients. She just hoped Alex Bowen saw it that way, too, rather than as a jumped-up temp interfering with his practice.

Alex. She had to stop thinking of him. For goodness' sake, a man that gorgeous had probably been snapped up since the age of twelve. And even if he wasn't, she was in no position to do anything about it.

'I'll see you in a fortnight, then,' she said to Mrs Martin.

'Right you are, Doctor.'

Two prescriptions for the Pill, one newborn colic, a mole that might or might not be pre-cancerous and needed referring to the local hospital, a case of persistent athlete's foot, two postnatal checks and a patient with mild depression meant that the rest of the morning flew by and Tina managed to push Alex completely from her mind. At precisely ten minutes to twelve, she finished typing the last of her notes into the practice computer system, logged out, tidied her desk and put the now heavy collecting tin in her bag.

And collided with Alex as she walked out of the door.

He was completely solid. Not a hint of flab anywhere. Like granite. Definitely Heathcliff, she thought.

'I'm sorry,' she said, taking a step back. 'I...' Her voice faded. What was there to say? She hadn't been looking where she was going and had cannoned into him. But there was no damage done—no one had dropped a file or spilled coffee or hurt themselves. 'I'm sorry,' she said again.

He looked pointedly at his watch. 'Off already?'

Was he accusing her of clock-watching—of skiving off early? She was about to tell him where to go, then remembered who he was. And he'd only just got back, according to Maggie, so he probably didn't know the full story yet. 'In accordance with my agreed hours, yes,' she said carefully.

'What about afternoon surgery?'

She shook her head. Hadn't Maggie told him she was part time? 'I work mornings only. And, if you'll excuse me, I really need to go.' Because she was going to be late. 'I have an appointment.' Picking up Josh, actually, but there was no time for a full explanation. And she didn't want to see the judgement, the pity in his eyes when she told him that Josh had ADHD, attention-deficit hyperactivity disorder, and was on transitional arrangements to ease him into school.

Though at least, being a doctor, Alex wouldn't come out with the usual spiel about how she really ought to watch Josh's diet and make sure he didn't eat anything containing E-numbers; or how Ritalin, the stimulant drug used to treat the condition, was really bad for children because it was related to speed; or how ADHD didn't exist, Josh was only like it because she let him watch too much television. Phrases that even now pressed all her buttons and sent her blood pressure and her temperature soaring and made her want to give the so-called concerned person a lecture about basic neurology and dopamine receptors.

Just as Alex was about to probe further, there was a cry from the waiting room. 'Help! Somebody, help!'

As one, they walked swiftly into the waiting room, where an elderly woman was lying on the floor.

'Ruby Parker. She was due to see me for a blood-pressure check—she has hypertension,' Alex said in an undertone.

'I'll ask Lorraine to clear the room, give her some privacy,' Tina said, while Alex went straight over to the old woman to examine her.

'She's— I think she's fainted—one minute she was talking to me and then she just collapsed,' the young woman by her side said, her voice rising into hysteria. 'She said her leg felt funny, and then she was on the floor.'

'Did she say anything about dizziness? Or seeing spots in front of her eyes?' Tina asked as she returned from her hasty confab with the receptionist.

'Gran said she'd had spots in front of her eyes first thing, but everything was all right by the time I came to pick her up.' The young woman wrung her hands together. 'Mum'll never forgive me if anything happens.'

'You're in the right place,' Tina said gently. 'Don't worry, we'll sort it all out.'

Alex was checking the old lady's pulse and respiration, frowning slightly.

'TIA?' she asked him, using the shorthand for transient ischaemic attack—commonly known as a mini-stroke. It happened when a small blood clot got stuck in a blood vessel in the brain, and could sometimes cause a sudden blackout like the one Ruby Parker had just suffered.

Sometimes vision, speech and sensation were impaired, but everything usually cleared up within twenty-four hours and the patient was fine again. The bad news was, the patient's risk of suffering a full stroke or a heart attack increased after a TIA.

'Probably,' he said. 'Gemma, has your gran had anything like this before?'

The young woman shook her head. 'I dunno. You'd have to ask Mum.'

'Where—? What's happened?' the old lady quavered.

'Easy, now, Mrs Parker,' Alex said, relieved that at least she hadn't lost her ability to communicate, known as aphasia. It was looking more like a TIA than a full stroke. 'You blacked out. Did you bang your head at all?'

'No.'

'Does anywhere hurt?' he asked, checking for the possibility of broken bones.

'No, but I can't move my arm,' she said, panic rising in her voice.

'That sometimes happens,' Tina reassured her as she and Alex helped the old lady to sit up, 'but you'll get the movement back. We think you might have had a minor stroke. Has anything like this happened before? Spots before your eyes, feeling dizzy, blacking out?'

'I get spots before my eyes most days,' Ruby told her. 'I'm used to it. Nothing to bother about.'

Alex and Tina exchanged a telling glance. There was everything to worry about, from the sound of it. The more episodes of TIA a patient suffered, the greater the risk of a full stroke or a heart attack. Together, they helped her to her feet and slowly walked her into Alex's consulting room, followed by Gemma, who was still wringing her hands.

'I'm going to send you for some tests today, Mrs

Parker,' Alex said as they settled her into a chair. 'Some blood tests and a scan.' Tina knew exactly what he meant. A CT scan to check for narrowed arteries and blood tests to check for any clotting abnormalities, to see just how close Ruby was to having a stroke. 'In the meantime, you'll need to take an aspirin a day.' The aspirin reduced the stickiness of the platelets in the blood, so Ruby wouldn't have the same problems with blood clots.

'You mean I've got to go to hospital? But I—I can't! How do I get—?'

'I'll take you, Gran,' Gemma told her.

'But I'm all right now. I don't need to go to hospital.'

'We need you checked out, Mrs Parker,' Alex said gently. 'I'll go and make some calls, and they should be able to fit you in this afternoon.'

'And I'll get you a glass of water,' Tina added. On her way back from the water fountain, she glanced at the surgery clock and could have howled. She was going to be really, *really* late. Maybe she should ask Lorraine to ring the school and let them know she was on her way.

But Alex pre-empted her as she walked in the door. 'Thank you for your help, Dr Lawson. You have an appointment, I believe.'

'Yes—yes, I do.' Why did he have to make her feel so guilty about it? 'But I'm leaving you in the best possible hands, Mrs Parker.' And for the best of reasons. So why did she feel as if she was letting everyone down?

CHAPTER TWO

'MUMMY, Mummy!' Josh, who'd been sitting on the bench in the cloakroom and tapping his feet while he waited for his mother, leapt up and ran straight over to her, cannoning into her and wrapping his arms round her legs at the same time. 'I thought you were *never* going to come!'

From long practice, Tina managed to keep her balance. Just. 'Hello, gorgeous,' she said, hugging her son. 'I'm sorry, I was held up at work.' She looked over at Donna, Josh's learning support worker. 'Emergency,' she mouthed. Donna smiled back, reassuring her. 'Have you had a nice morning?' she asked Josh.

'I got a sticker. Look!'

Tina admired the 'I did good work' badge. 'Well done, you! What did you get it for?'

'I drew a picture. It was all about Peter Pan. I drew his shadow, and Tinkerbell, and Captain Hook, and Nana the dog. Can we have a dog?'

'Not just now, honey.'

'Jay's got a dog.'

'I know.' She changed the subject swiftly, hoping the promise would be enough to distract him from the dog. She'd love a dog, too, but there was a 'no pets' clause in their tenancy agreement. Until she'd regrouped, she couldn't afford to buy their own house, so that meant no dogs. 'Shall we go to the park after lunch?'

'Oh, yes! Yes, *please*!' Josh whooped and ran round her in a circle.

'How's he been today?' she asked.

'Excited. It's the hair thing,' Donna explained. Her hair, usually clipped back in a sensible ponytail, was in half a dozen punk-style bunches, festooned with brightly coloured clips. 'He managed four minutes in circle time.'

Last Friday, it had been ten. One step forward, two steps back, Tina thought. You never knew from one day to the next whether Josh would feel 'calm like a swan' or 'fizzy like a firework', as he put it.

'But he sat nicely to do his bookwork and he had a good playtime.'

Tina ruffled his hair. 'Well done.' She looked at Donna. 'Any homework?'

'A new reading book, plus the high-frequency words list again. He managed six today.'

When Tina had tested him, last night, he'd known all eighteen. She forced a smile, reminding herself not to hold Josh's good days against him. Just because he could do it once, that didn't mean he could do it all the time. 'We'll keep going. Ready for lunch, Josh?'

'I'm *starving*!' Josh stopped circling her and took his schoolbag from his peg. 'Bye, Mrs Ellis!'

'Hey, Josh. Remember, we walk nicely through school,' Tina said, seeing her son prepare to race through the door. 'And there's a road outside. So what does that mean?'

'We walk sensibly,' Josh said, his blue eyes dancing with mischief. 'We can play Peter Pan. You can be Tinkerbell.'

Tina thought of her generous curves, and grinned. 'I'm hardly fairy-like.'

'You can be Captain Hook, then. Come on! Let's be pirates!'

'Here's the deal. Lunch, words, then pirates in the park.'

'That's brilliant! I really, *really* love you, Mummy.' He wrapped his arms round her in a fierce bear hug.

'And I love you, too.' Tina hugged him back, tears pricking the backs of her eyes. To have him happy and settled like this meant more to her than anything. Even better, she could do the job she loved here, too—and since this morning she had another three months' grace before she had to look for another locum position and hope that the new surgery wouldn't be too far away from Josh's school so she could fit her work round his timetable.

And she wouldn't even let herself think about how she was going to cope with the long summer holidays—they were still months away. And time didn't go that fast…did it?

Two days later, she concluded it did. Alex had only been back in the surgery since Monday morning and already it felt like she'd been working with him for ever. But not a nice kind of for ever: the rapport between them when they'd helped Ruby Parker had dissolved almost instantly when he'd reminded her that she had 'an appointment'.

Maybe he was one of those people who didn't think you should mix children and a career—that you should be a dedicated doctor, full stop. Well, she thought differently. Being a mother had made her far more aware of her patients' feelings, and that made her a better family doctor. If he gave her the chance, she'd prove the argument.

The worst thing was, she was so *aware* of him. She knew the second he walked into the surgery. It was as if there was some weird magnetic force between them and her body reacted instantly, her fingers tingling with adrenalin and her pulse speeding up. And that was with brick walls between them. When he was in the same room as her, it felt as if someone had lit a thousand tiny sparklers. She'd barely been able to concentrate at the usual Wednesday morning staff meeting, she'd been trying so hard not to stare at him and drool. And she hadn't exactly contributed much to the discussion which, no doubt, had convinced Alex even more that she was a dead loss to the surgery.

Damn, damn and double damn. Alex was one of the most attractive men she'd ever met. And that included Rod, she thought with a flood of guilt. Rod had been dead little more than a year and here she was, mooning over another man like a lovesick adolescent.

'What kind of woman are you?' she asked herself crossly. 'Playing the merry widow—it's not on. Be *sensible*.'

And sensible meant not acting on the attraction between them.

For a start, they had a professional relationship—even if it was only for as long as she was his locum—and the slightest hint of anything personal would spoil that.

Secondly, there was Rod. She couldn't betray his memory by falling for another man so soon.

Thirdly, and most importantly, there was Josh. Tina's first duty was to him. He'd already had so much upheaval in his young life. She wasn't going to add to it by having an affair that couldn't possibly go anywhere, no matter how desirable she found Alex.

Maybe it was time for her to leave.

Maybe Alex would ask her to leave anyway.

As if on cue, there was a knock at her door and it opened enough for Alex to look through. 'Can I have a word?' As if he guessed she was about to cite the fact that the Wednesday staff meeting had overrun slightly and she really needed to see her next patient, Alex added, 'This won't take a minute.'

She nodded, trying to control the sudden fluttering in her stomach. What was it about him? Those eyes, that mouth, the rich timbre of his voice... She reminded herself to be professional as he walked in. This was work. Not pleasure. And she wasn't going to embarrass either of them by throwing herself at him.

She put on her best doctor's voice. 'How can I help?'

There was an odd look on his face and she flushed spectacularly. Her hair. It had to be. He could hardly miss it. 'It was supposed to wash out,' she muttered. It had—to some extent. It was only when she'd reread the instructions on the side of the can that she'd seen the words. *Do not use on coloured hair.* Which included highlights. Which was why her fringe still had obvious purple streaks after ten washes. 'My hairdresser's going to colour it back later in the week.' Denise, her friend and hairdresser, had been convulsed with laughter when Tina had rung her to explain the problem and beg her to turn her hair back to its normal colour.

Amusement flickered briefly at the corner of his mouth. 'It's not the hair, oh, sober Dr Lawson.'

He'd remembered her words with embarrassing accuracy and she squirmed inwardly.

'I've come to apologise, actually—Maggie put me straight about your arrangement with us. I'm sorry I leapt to conclusions the other day.' His cheeks went faintly pink. 'We've been unlucky with some of our locums in the past. I shouldn't have let that cloud my judgement.'

She spread her hands. 'That's OK.' This was his practice and she was just a locum. He didn't *have* to apologise. Though it warmed her that he had. 'It's half my fault, too, because I was late for picking up Josh and there wasn't time to explain properly.'

'The fault, my dear Dr Lawson, is all mine.' He gave her an exaggerated bow to match the exaggeratedly courteous words and she was very glad she wasn't standing up. Because the old-fashioned gesture—even if he was hamming it up deliberately to defuse any potential tension between them—turned her legs to jelly. 'And I wanted to thank you for picking up some problems with my patients in my absence—diagnosing Lizzy Riley with diabetes, for one.'

Anyone in her position would have picked it up. The cut that refused to heal, feeling tired, needing to go to the loo more often, slightly blurred vision—symptoms that had come on gradually. Plus, Lizzy had admitted cheerfully that she knew she was overweight but was hopeless at dieting. Tina had checked Lizzy's feet to discover what she'd half suspected—a small sore. They were typical symptoms of late onset diabetes and a simple blood test had confirmed the diagnosis, enabling Tina to prescribe oral hypoglycaemics and a careful diet for Lizzy, with strict instructions to take the tablets regularly and call Tina if she felt sick or had a headache.

Why was he making such a big deal about it? 'I *am* a qualified doctor,' she said crossly.

'But not all locums take this amount of care with patients.'

'I wouldn't dare do otherwise. I grew up round here,' she reminded him.

'Yes.' He paused. 'Are you busy tonight?'

Her eyes widened. Was he asking her out? 'I—'

'If you're not,' he continued, as if she hadn't stumbled over the beginnings of a refusal, 'I'd like to talk to you. Perhaps we could go for a drink this evening?'

Alex hadn't meant to say that at all. He could do all this through Maggie, the practice manager; he didn't need to get involved. In any sense. He didn't *want* to get involved with anyone. Not after Vivi. That was why he'd taken a vow of celibacy before he'd come to Ellingthorpe, nearly six years ago, and had stuck to it despite the best efforts of the mothers in the village to interest him in their eligible daughters. He'd made senior partner at such a young age because he'd recognised he was no good at relationships and had spent the time and energy on his career instead.

But Tina did something to him, something he couldn't explain. Something that made him want to break every rule in the book, and then some. He'd never felt like this before, even with Vivi. And it wasn't because he was looking for another Vivi. Vivi was tall, blonde and slender; Tina had light brown highlighted hair, was of average height and very curvy. Vivi was always laughing, always touching people on their hands or shoulders or arms, hugging people; Tina was a little more serious and reserved, with a hint of mischief lurking in those stunning violet-blue eyes. Vivi was in his past. And Tina...

He couldn't get Tina out of his mind. Especially since Maggie had filled him in on a very important detail. Tina was a single parent—which meant his unbreakable rule about married women didn't apply to her.

And the mischievous imp had taken full advantage of the fact, grabbing control of his mouth and asking her out.

She'd refuse. She was bound to.

'I'm sorry.' She spread her hands. Lord, she had beautiful hands. Sensible family GP's hands, clean and scrubbed with no nail varnish. And yet her fingers were slender, the shape of her nails a perfect oval, and he itched to feel those hands twining through his hair, massaging his scalp as his mouth…

He became aware that she was speaking and his body was just—only just—under control.

'Josh.'

Her little boy. *Leave it there.*

But the imp had other ideas. 'Could you get a babysitter?'

'I prefer not to leave Josh.'

Really leave it, he told himself fiercely. She obviously doesn't want to know—she's being polite and you're pushing too hard.

Again, the imp refused to listen. 'Then perhaps I could come over to your place instead?'

There was a long, long pause while he convinced himself that she'd find an excuse and he'd somehow manage to retrieve both his common sense and this situation and kick the imp into touch.

'If your wife doesn't mind.'

Ex-wife, actually. And she hadn't given a damn, in the end. 'I'm not married.'

And then she nodded. 'All right.'

A heartbeat passed and the imp strutted his stuff, punching his arm in the air and yelling, 'Yes! Re-ee-*sult*!' For one horrible moment Alex thought *he'd* actually done it, too. But Tina wasn't looking shocked or surprised. So he was safe…this time. 'I don't want to interfere with Josh's bedtime routine, so what time does he go to bed?'

'Half past eight.'

'OK. I'll see you at a quarter to nine, then?'

'A quarter to nine,' she agreed.

Tina stared after Alex as he closed the door. Had she gone stark, staring mad? This was crazy. Completely and utterly crazy. She should stop it right now. Why on earth had she agreed to a date with her boss—and on her own territory at that?

Business, she told herself firmly. It was business, not a date.

And yet there had been something in those beautiful dark eyes…

'Absolutely not. You imagined the whole thing, Tina Lawson. It's work and that's all,' she said loudly.

On his side, at least. And it ought to be on hers.

Oh, why had she made that stupid comment about his wife? He must have thought that she was fishing for information, maybe even trying to see where she'd fit into his life—he might even have thought she was giving him the come-on! She was definitely going to die of embarrassment the next time she saw him.

And she really had to grab Maggie and ask her to fill her in properly. How come a man as gorgeous as Alex wasn't married?

Well, there was an obvious answer. Maybe he was gay, so he wasn't interested in women. But if that were the case, why had he looked at her like that, stared at her mouth as if he'd wanted to kiss her?

Or was that wishful thinking because she'd wanted to kiss him?

She pulled herself together then paged Lorraine to let her know that she was ready for her next patient.

'Hello, Jan. How are you?' she asked as her patient walked in.

'OK.'

Tina picked up the momentary hesitation. 'Jan, if you're worried about having the Triple Test, you don't *have* to have it. It's a screening test and it's your choice whether to have it or not.' The simple blood test screened babies for the risk of spina bifida and Down's syndrome. Sixteen weeks into a pregnancy was the optimum time to do the test, which was the reason for Jan's appointment today. Tina had discussed it with Jan at her previous antenatal appointment, saying that the results weren't conclusive—they just gave you a probability of the risk of your baby having a problem. If the risk was below one in two hundred, she'd be offered an amniocentesis which could give her a definite answer.

'I hate needles,' Jan said with a wry grimace.

Tina grinned. 'It's nothing compared to the ones you've already faced!' Tina knew that Jan's much-wanted pregnancy was the result of her third cycle of IVF treatment—the last she and her husband had been able to go through for emotional reasons as well as financial. 'Now, this won't hurt a bit.'

The blood test over, Jan visibly relaxed.

'I ought to offer you a sweetie for being brave,' Tina teased.

'If it's chocolate, the answer's yes,' Jan teased back.

Tina fished in her bottom drawer and handed Jan a wrapped chocolate. 'Don't tell anyone else about my secret stash, OK? They all think I just have kiddy sweets.' She winked. 'Anything else you'd like to discuss?'

'Well…it's probably nothing.'

'But you're going to tell me anyway,' Tina said. 'You're not making a fuss—my job's to reassure you if you're worried.'

'It's just…the itching,' Jan confessed. 'I know your skin's supposed to change in pregnancy, but I wasn't expecting this.'

It was too early for obstetric cholestasis—the classic signs of itching started at around twenty-eight weeks—

but Tina wasn't going to take any chances. 'Is the itch anywhere in particular?'

'My hands.' Almost as if talking about it had triggered the itch, Jan began to scratch the backs of her hands. 'And my ankles.'

Classic symptoms—but the timing was wrong. 'Let's have a look at you.' Tina pulled the curtains around the bed, giving Jan privacy to slip off her skirt and blouse, then examined her patient. 'Hmm. I don't think it's obstetric cholestasis—that's a liver condition in pregnancy that tends to make you itch—because I've never known a case this early on. But I'll take some blood for a test anyway.' Then she noticed Jan's high colour. 'Jan—forgive me for asking, but are your cheeks usually this red?'

'No.'

Tina thought quickly. Jan was a classroom assistant at Ellingthorpe Primary—and Josh had said something about some children in his class not being well. Maybe… 'Is anything going round at school?'

Jan shrugged. 'A bit of slapped cheek, that's all.'

Slapped cheek—also known as fifth disease or erythema infectiosum—was a common childhood infection caused by erythrovirus B19, previously called parvovirus. Outbreaks tended to occur in the spring, building up to a peak every four years. Affected children had the bright red cheeks which gave the disease its nickname plus a high temperature, followed by an itchy, blotchy or lacy rash all over the body which lasted for up to two weeks and which could flare up again even months later in hot weather or on sunny days. In most children, it was harmless, but it was dangerous for children who had blood disorders such as sickle cell anaemia.

And it could be dangerous to pregnant women, particularly those in the first trimester.

Jan was in the second trimester and the risk was smaller, but it was enough to worry Tina. Half of all adults were immune; less than a third of those who caught it passed it on to the baby. But a small proportion of babies went on to develop severe anaemia, and the risk of a resulting miscarriage was greater before twenty weeks.

'Jan, have you had a rash at all? Or any joint pains?' Tina asked when her patient was dressed again and seated by her desk.

'I've ached a bit, but that's all.'

'I think you've got slapped cheek.'

Jan's eyes widened. 'Is that dangerous? For the baby, I mean?'

'Only in a very few cases. Most babies are absolutely fine. But I'll take a blood test and send you for a scan anyway, just to be on the safe side.' First-time mums didn't usually feel the baby moving until around twenty weeks, so Tina couldn't check whether the baby's pattern of movements had changed. But there was one thing she could do to reassure Jan. She took the Sonicaid from her drawer. 'If you'd like to get back on the couch and bare your tummy for me again, we'll have a listen to the baby's heartbeat.' She picked up the tube of jelly used to magnify the signals. 'This is cold, I'm afraid—the only place you'll get it warmed up is at Melbury General,' she warned as she squeezed the jelly onto Jan's stomach. As soon as she pressed the head of the receiver onto the jelly, they could hear a reassuring tick-tock from the monitor. 'That's your heartbeat,' she said with a smile, moving the receiver round a bit. 'Here we are. One baby.' The heartbeat was quieter, but also quicker, somewhere around one hundred and forty beats a minute.

'Well, it sounds all right,' Jan said, visibly relieved.

Tina hid her worry and handed Jan a wad of tissues to

clean the remaining jelly from her stomach. 'I'll just ring through and get you an appointment for a scan.' When she'd finished the call, she turned to Jan. 'They'll see you tomorrow afternoon at 3:40.'

'Thanks, Dr Lawson.'

'Any time.' Tina smiled back at her. 'Take care, and I'll see you in four weeks.'

CHAPTER THREE

BEFORE Tina knew it, it was a quarter to twelve. She logged off the computer system, said goodbye to Lorraine and ran up the hill to school. Josh had had a good day—Donna had only had to take him out of PE twice instead of the usual five or six times—but their planned afternoon in the garden attacking the weeds was ruined by rain, and Josh was nearly climbing the walls by teatime. Only an hour playing in the bath, with plenty of top-ups to stop the water becoming completely freezing, mollified him. Half the bathwater ended up on the bathroom floor and Tina had only just finished mopping up the lino after Josh's bedtime story when the doorbell rang.

She stopped dead.

Alex.

His visit had been at the back of her mind—oh, who was she trying to kid? It had been at the forefront of her mind for most of the day, ever since he'd suggested it. She'd found herself agonising over what to wear—she, Tina Lawson, who never fussed about primping and preening and make-up! Worse still, she'd found herself thinking about him at odd moments during the day. Wondering. Imagining that beautiful, sensual mouth touching hers. Guessing how his skin would feel against hers.

This was utterly ridiculous. They'd known each other three days, that was all.

Long enough to know, her heart whispered.

It's not going to happen, her mind insisted firmly. You know the reasons why. Josh, work, Rod. Remember that.

Three little words, all with one syllable and less than five letters. It isn't hard.

Oh, but it is, her heart complained. *Way too hard.*

She'd been sidetracked by Josh's bath this evening but Alex must be early. He had to be. No way was it already a quarter to nine. She had plenty of time to tidy up the house, change her scruffy jeans and T-shirt that had seen better days for something more professional, create the right impression… It couldn't be that late. It couldn't be.

The clock in the hall said otherwise.

Oh, great. The house was a complete tip and she looked a mess—she hadn't even had time to brush her hair! It was hardly going to endear her to her boss. Especially when he looked so cool and together, she thought when she opened the door.

'Hi.'

Even dressed casually in chinos, a crew-neck olive-green cotton sweater and desert boots, he exuded authority and competence. Not to mention sex. That voice just made her melt.

Stop it, she told herself. This is business.

Wanna bet? asked her heart.

Tina raked a hand through her hair in a vain attempt to restore order to it. 'I, um… Come in.' Her flush deepened when she led him into the living room. Lego and books were scattered everywhere—Josh definitely hadn't earned a star on his chart for tidying up tonight—and stones, Josh's current obsession, were piled on the window-sill. Embarrassed, she cleared a chair for Alex.

'I brought this.' He handed her a chilled bottle wrapped in tissue paper.

'Thanks. I'll get some glasses.' The narrow galley kitchen was tidier than the living room, but only just. The plates, cutlery and pans were stacked, ready to be washed, yet it still looked a bit of a state. Alex must be ruing the day Maggie had taken her on, she thought miserably as she placed the bottle on the table and hunted through the kitchen drawer for a corkscrew.

Was this what life would have been like with Bethany? Alex wondered. Toys everywhere, drawings Blu-tacked proudly to the walls? He was shocked to find that he could barely remember what it had been like after his daughter's birth. Had their house been full of musical toys, mobiles, playmats and baby gyms?

He shut the thoughts off quickly. That wasn't why he was here. He forced himself to study the space collage—the planets were definitely recognisable as Jupiter with its red spot and Saturn with its rings, there was a piece of string attaching the astronaut to his space ship, and the tail of the comet sparkled with silver and gold glitter. The whole picture oozed exuberance, from the stars cut out from purple hologram paper to the huge smile drawn on the astronaut's tinfoil space helmet. Purple was clearly Josh's favourite colour.

He knew he was being nosy and should stop right there, but he couldn't help reading the star chart next to it. Monday and Tuesday had stars for tidying up toys before bed—today's square was very obviously blank. All three days had a star for taking fish oil without a fuss, and Monday's squares were completely filled, with additional stars for number-work and reading. And, he noticed with a smile, each day had a star added 'for being gorgeous'. Josh was clearly very much loved.

A love he'd always looked for and never really known.

'It's just a star chart,' a voice said behind him, and he whipped round, embarrassed at being caught prying.

'Sorry. I shouldn't have been poking about.'

Tina shrugged and handed him a glass of the Chablis he'd brought. 'No problem.'

Their hands touched for an instant and the glass would have fallen if he hadn't tightened his fingers round it. I'm not imagining it, he thought, as he watched her eyes darken, the pupils expand. *It's real.* And she feels it too.

Her hands were shaking. And her voice wasn't much better. 'Sorry it's such a mess in here. Wet play.'

'Of course.'

She's the one. Don't blow it. Kiss the girl, said the imp.

Back off, said his common sense. And it's too early to tell.

No, it's not. She's the one. Kiss her, the imp insisted.

There was a brief tussle between the two, and the imp subsided, sulking. There was a long and very awkward silence…

And then Tina burst out laughing. 'Shall we start all this again?'

Her smile was infectious. 'Sure. Is this an OK time for you to talk to me?'

She nodded. 'Josh is in bed. Not asleep, and he'll probably come downstairs in a minute with the feeblest of excuses, but he's in bed.' She cleared a space for herself on the sofa—the furthest possible space away from the chair she'd cleared for him, Alex noticed. As if she didn't trust herself to sit near him. Or maybe his thoughts were written all over his face and she didn't trust him.

The imp had stopped sulking, encouraged by her smile, and was yelling at Alex to scoop her up and sit her on his lap—but he managed to resist the urge. Too fast, too soon. He needed to give her time to get to know him— give *himself* time to get to know *her*. He was too old and too sensible to act on a bad case of lust.

Don't bet on it, warned the imp.

'It's not usually this much of a tip in here. And I'm neat at work,' Tina said.

'I know. Maggie speaks highly of you, the others have all said how well you fit in, and the patients are full of how good "our Tina" is.'

'But?'

'Are you always this in-your-face, or is it just with me?'

She sighed. 'Sorry. I seem to spend half my life apologising and the other half on the defensive.' She turned the glass round in her hands. 'I guess what I'm trying to say is that you have to take me as you find me.'

Take her… The imp rubbed his hands together and conjured up a vision of Tina, her hair equally tousled, lying naked between crumpled sheets on his bed. Alex's stomach tightened. No. It would be fatal to start thinking of her like that. Or why those sheets would be crumpled. Or how that soft mouth would feel against his, swollen and tender from kissing him.

'I…' Too late. His imagination had already gone into overdrive, making his throat dry and his body surge. 'I wanted to talk to you about the website.'

'I'm sorry. I should have cleared it with you first.'

He shook his head. 'Maggie's the practice manager. If she agreed it with the others, that's good enough for me. But we ought to be paying you for it.'

She shrugged. 'It keeps my hand in. And it's useful on my CV.'

'Mum-*mee*!' The call came loudly from upstairs.

Tina rolled her eyes and stood up; she placed her glass on the mantelpiece. 'Sorry. I'll only be a minute.'

Alex sat patiently waiting for her, and then his eye was caught by the framed photograph next to her glass. Tina was laughing, her arm around the waist of a tall, sandy-haired man who was clearly Josh's father—the small sandy-haired boy sitting on his shoulders wore an identical smile. They were obviously happy together—something drastic must have happened to turn Tina into a single parent. Something as drastic as his own experience with Vivi perhaps? It was no wonder Tina could be prickly and defensive. He immediately felt guilty for pushing her. And even guiltier at the thought that she could catch him prying again. Hurriedly, he sat down again and concentrated on his wine.

'He wanted a drink,' Tina explained as she came back into the living room. 'And another story.' Her smile was wry. 'It was the only way I could stop him coming down here and pestering you with a million and one questions, or telling you his banana joke.'

'The banana joke you've heard a thousand times a day? It's tough, being a single parent,' he said softly.

Her chin lifted a fraction. 'It doesn't affect the way I do my job.'

'I know. If anything, you understand the pressures on some of our patients more than anyone else at the practice.' He paused. 'I notice you've started a group for parents of children with learning difficulties.'

Her eyes narrowed as she tried to decode his words. 'Are you asking me about Josh?'

'I—'

'Because, if you are, Maggie clearly hasn't filled you in yet and you'd better know everything.' She folded her arms. 'Josh has ADHD but I don't want that to define him. He's a very bright, funny, capable little boy with a lot going for him. He just has problems sitting still and concentrating, and he finds group work difficult.'

'Hence the star chart.' Because small, frequent rewards worked best for ADHD children.

'And that's why I'm part time—he's on a transitional

entry to school, and his hours are increasing as he can cope with them. I love my job and I'm a hundred per cent dedicated to it during my working hours, but I need to be there for Josh outside school and that's my first priority.'

'That's completely understandable,' he reassured her, 'and no one at the practice will have a problem with that.'

She looked at him as if she couldn't quite take his words at face value. Josh's father had clearly hurt her very much, damaging her capacity to trust, he thought. 'You're from round here originally, aren't you?'

Tina nodded. 'Though I trained in London and I liked working there. Then Josh came along. We'd thought for a while we ought to move out of London, for his sake...' She shrugged. 'Josh wasn't settling at school, so I decided to come home to Ellingthorpe. I know the area and my parents are here, so it's easier if I need help.'

There was obviously a lot she wasn't telling him. 'Is Josh on Ritalin?'

She shook her head. 'Too young.' The stimulant drug wasn't generally prescribed for children under six. 'And he's not that bad—somewhere in the middle of the scale, really. The consultant says it's best if we can try to keep going with one-to-one support at school.'

'I saw on the chart you're giving him fish oil. Has it made any difference?'

'It's too early to say—he's still on the triple dose until his LCP stores are built up.' LCPs, long-chain polyunsaturated fatty acids, had been shown to help development of the eye and brain, particularly in the areas of concentration, memory and learning ability, and the eicosapentaenoic acid or EPA in fish oil was thought to help communication between the nerve-endings in the brain. 'But I'm hoping it might kick in when we've passed the twelve-week mark.'

'What about homeopathy?'

She stared at him in utter shock, as if he'd already been described to her as a dyed-in-the-wool traditionalist, someone who believed all complementary medicine was pure quackery.

'No. He's seeing a cranial osteopath in Melbury, though—Dan Bridges.'

Cranial osteopathy could make a difference to some children, possibly through helping them to relax. 'Dan's very good. And I can give you the details of a good local homeopath, if you ever want to give it a try,' Alex said.

'Thanks.'

So now he knew about Josh. But it didn't tell him what he *really* wanted to know—where the sandy-haired man fitted in. He couldn't stop himself asking. 'How does Josh's father feel about you moving here?'

For a moment, her violet-blue eyes sparkled with tears. 'He died, six months before Josh started school.' She swallowed hard. 'Which was why I had to move.'

But…hadn't she said she'd moved *after* Josh had started school?

And she was very close to tears. It was all his fault. He'd seen the photograph, it had told him all he needed to know. He shouldn't have pushed her for more. Reacting purely on instinct, Alex put down his glass, brushed the Lego off the sofa next to her, sat down and put his arm round her. 'Hey, it's OK. If you don't want to talk about it, that's fine.'

'No, you might as well know the whole story. Rod was an actor. He—he'd gone for an audition. I was working so I wasn't able to go with him for once. He said I brought him luck. Maybe if I'd switched duty, gone with him…' She choked back a sob. 'He didn't even get to the audition. The car's driver was still high as a kite from the stuff he'd taken at a club the night before and he went straight over a crossing. Rod didn't stand a chance. The police said it—it would have been quick, he wouldn't have known anything.'

How wrong he'd been—Josh's father hadn't hurt her at all. It was his *loss* that had crushed her. She was a doctor and she was so sure that if she'd been there, she'd have been able to save him. Alex knew that without having to look in her face—he'd done the same himself. Gone over and over it. If only he'd been there, it would have made a difference. He could have saved Bethany. If only he hadn't gone to that conference. If only... But it probably wouldn't have changed a thing. That was the worst thing. Knowing that you *should* have been able to make a difference—but when it came down to it you wouldn't have been able to. He tightened his hold, reassuring her.

'How old was Josh at the time?'

'Nearly four. And that's when all the behaviour problems blew up. I put it down to him being upset about losing his dad, but the nursery said it had been going on for months before that. He'd always been lively, a busy toddler who climbed everything in sight and was never still for a moment. I thought maybe they weren't handling him properly. Sometimes you have to pull rank with him. Then it got worse when he started school. He was diagnosed with ADHD and I...came home.'

'Must have been hard.'

Tina pulled a face. 'We needed to find somewhere else to live anyway.'

'Why?' The question was out before he could stop it.

'The house was in Rod's name. And we'd...never got round to actually getting married.'

Which explained the lack of a ring.

'He didn't want to get married without his parents there.'

Alex frowned. 'Were they living abroad?'

She shook her head. 'Forty minutes away on the tube. It was my fault. They…didn't approve of me.' The words tumbled out in a rush. 'We met as students. Rod was reading law—he was supposed to join the family firm when he graduated. Except he hated being a lawyer. He'd always wanted to act. I told him to follow his dream and he switched his course to drama. He was good, really good, and he was happy. But his parents couldn't forgive me for tempting him away from their plans. And they had a point. If I hadn't interfered, he'd be a lawyer—and he'd still be alive now.'

'You don't know that. Accidents happen.' He paused. 'And babies often help mend relationships.'

'Not this one. Which was my fault, of course, because they felt I didn't discipline Josh properly and he was just a naughty boy who needed taking in hand.' She sighed. 'I think Rod knew his parents weren't ever going to come round to us being together. He said we should get married anyway, but by then it felt too much like making a state-ment. So we left it.' She bit her lip. 'We never got round to making wills. Something else was always more ur-gent—an audition, an exam, an emergency at the surgery. The house should probably have gone to Josh, but Rod's parents were lawyers—they had all the arguments.'

'Couldn't they have at least sold you the house?'

There was a tinge of bitterness in her smile this time. 'Josh or the house. My choice.'

'They were going to demand custody unless you didn't contest the house?' he asked, shocked.

'Clearly I wasn't a good parent. Josh was going off the rails, and I was a slattern.' She gestured to the mess in the living room. 'I'd be lying if I said this wasn't typical, though I generally have a blitz before I go to bed and I'm trying to teach Josh to be tidier. But a happy child's more important to me than a spotless house. Do the dusting or play with my son—well, my choice wasn't theirs.' She shrugged. 'House prices went crazy in London. I couldn't afford the going rate, even though Mum and Dad offered to lend me some money, so I moved back here. I'm renting at the moment, but that doesn't mean I'll do a flit with some bloke and let you down. Josh needs a lot of attention and, most of all, security. So we're staying put.'

Effectively warning him off, Alex thought. Josh came first and she wasn't going to risk a relationship with *any-one*. 'I realise that,' he said softly. He wanted to keep holding her close. Having her in his arms was doing in-sane things to his heartbeat and the imp was whispering all sorts of suggestions in his ear. *Kiss her. Brush her hair back from her face and kiss her.* But he knew that Tina wasn't ready to move on. He had to back off. Now. Gently, he removed his arm.

She rubbed a hand across her eyes. 'I'm sorry. I didn't mean to land all that on you.'

'Sounds to me as if you needed to talk.'

'If that's your bedside manner, no wonder your patients love you.'

Bedside manner.

The imp did a little shimmy of excitement.

Alex tried to rein himself back. It was a bad move, thinking about bed and Tina at the same time, especially as her thigh was only inches away from his own. He knew he wasn't in a position to offer her anything—he was a disaster area where relationships were concerned—and she clearly still needed time to grieve for Rod. And yet the thought wouldn't go away. Tina, in his bed, laughing

up at him the way she'd been laughing in that photograph,
her face full of love and happiness.

Except she never would look at him like that. Whatever
attraction was between them, she'd already made it clear
she wasn't going to act on it. And even if she changed
her mind, it could never be anything more than temporary.
Because when she got close, she'd realise that he was
basically unlovable. Just like Vivi had.

His expression must have told her that she'd just spoken aloud. 'Sorry. I didn't mean to say that about your
bedside manner. Oh, hell. I think you've just caught me
on a bad day. I'm normally more together than this.'

'We all have days like that.' He'd had enough of them
himself, days when he'd thought he'd go mad and
couldn't understand why he wasn't coping.

'And I've talked too much.' Tina raked a hand through
her hair. 'It wasn't supposed to be like this. You weren't
supposed to see this woman with purple hair who's in a
complete mess.'

'You're human, Tina.'

'I'm a *doctor*.'

'But you're also human. And you've been through a
tough time.' He paused. 'Look, I understand you have
family commitments. We'll be flexible if Josh needs you.
And I meant it about asking you to stay for another three
months. We need another full-time partner really, but it'll
take time to find someone suitable—a lot of newly qualified GPs prefer to work on a salary at a health centre,
not go into a practice.'

And clearly *she* wasn't suitable, Tina thought, so he
wasn't likely to offer her the job. Even if she could work
full time, she had Josh to think about. She couldn't take
any night calls and leave her son on his own. Right now,
her life was a mess. Even her own parents, kind and un-

derstanding though they were about Josh's condition, had said Josh was more than enough to keep her hands full.

Why couldn't she just cope on her own, like other single parents did?

She became aware that Alex was talking to her. 'Sorry, I didn't catch what you said.'

'I like what you've done with the surgery website. But I'll only let you continue with it—and the patient information sheets—if we pay you.' He named a sum that made her blink.

'I can't possibly take that much.'

'It's the going rate. I checked it out.'

He *would*, she thought ruefully.

'Deal?'

If she said no, he'd refuse to let her work on the website, and she *needed* that as career insurance, so if things didn't work out as a locum she could go to one of the big health organisations or magazines and offer her services as a medical journalist, working from home when Josh was at school. 'Deal,' she said faintly.

'Good.'

And then he lost his head completely. He could have shaken her hand, he could have just smiled and done nothing. But no... The imp whispered in his ear again. *Do it the old-fashioned way. Seal it with a kiss.*

He should have ignored the suggestion. But once the idea was in his head, he couldn't stop thinking about it. A light kiss. The merest touch of his lips against hers. No pressure. That was all he intended.

But it suddenly turned into a lot more than that.

Because her lips were warm and soft and inviting, responding to his. Just the merest response, but it was there.

He was shaking when he broke the kiss. She wasn't

unaffected either—her breathing was definitely quicker and her eyes were almost black, the pupils had expanded so much. He didn't dare let himself look too closely at the softness of her T-shirt. He was already close to losing his control, and seeing even the hint of a response from her breasts would be way too much for him.

'I'll see you tomorrow,' he said, trying and failing to inject some control into his voice. He sounded as husky as if he'd asked her to come to his bed, make love with him, unleash the passion that would drive away their respective demons.

Except they'd still be there in the morning. And he had to work with Tina, at least for the next three months. *Back off*, he reminded himself. 'I'll see myself out.'

Tina had no idea what she'd murmured to him as he left. Something inane, probably.

What the hell had she just done?

She'd let him kiss her, that's what. Worse, she'd kissed him back.

'You idiot,' she told herself. 'You've already been through this. You know why it can't happen. Do you really have to remind yourself yet again? Number one, he's your boss. Number two, even if he wasn't, you can't start a relationship and then bring Josh's world crashing down again when it ends—because, of course, it's going to end. And number three, there's Rod—how can you forget all he meant to you so quickly? It's barely a year since he died, it's disloyal to start even thinking about another man.' Let alone kiss one back.

She lifted a shaking hand to her mouth. Just a kiss. That's all it had been. Just a kiss. A way of sealing their deal. Nothing to get so hot and bothered about.

But that merest touch of his lips had made her extremely hot and bothered.

If she was honest, even before then he'd got under her skin. Tonight, she'd told him things she hadn't even told her best friend.

'You need your head examined. Now, stop skiving and get on with your work,' she told herself firmly, heading for the kitchen to make the dough for the cookies she'd promised to bake for the PTA coffee morning tomorrow, so it could firm up in the fridge while she blitzed the house, cleaned Josh's shoes and ironed his uniform—without even thinking of the rest of the ironing pile in the corner of her bedroom looming balefully at her every time she tried to ignore it. All she had to do was keep herself busy. Too busy to think of Alex Bowen. Because nothing, *nothing*, was going to come of this relationship.

CHAPTER FOUR

TINA dropped Josh off at school the next morning, delivered a large tin of home-made choc-chip cookies into the PTA chair's capable hands for the coffee morning, and was at her desk ten minutes before surgery began.

Then she saw the sticky note on the edge of her computer screen. Bright orange—she could hardly miss it—with clear, firm writing on it. *See me when you get in, please. AB.*

She went cold. Why? Had Alex had second thoughts about her being a locum here, now he'd seen what a mess she was outside work? Was it something to do with that kiss? Or…

Heart beating rapidly, she rapped on his door.

'Come in.'

'You wanted to see me?' The grimness in his face made her pulse accelerate even more.

'Sit down.'

She couldn't wait any longer. 'What's happened?'

'I had a call from Melbury General this morning about Jan Bailey. She had a miscarriage last night, and they're letting her go home today.'

Tina stared at him, aghast. 'Oh, no—that's terrible. Poor Jan. I saw her yesterday. I thought she might have slapped cheek, so I sent a blood sample to the lab and I got her an appointment for ultrasound this afternoon. I should have sent her straight to hospital—I *knew* it was an IVF baby.'

'It wouldn't have made any difference whether the baby

was IVF or naturally conceived. Viruses aren't fussy. You couldn't have prevented the miscarriage.'

'How do you *know* that?' she challenged.

'Tina, you did your best.'

'It wasn't good enough.'

'You did the same as every other GP in this practice would have done. So don't blame yourself—I just wanted you to hear the bad news from me, rather than through the grapevine in the village.'

'Thanks.' Tina bit her lip. 'I'll ask Mum to look after Josh so I can pop in to see her later.'

'You do that. Now, surgery calls.'

It was odd, she thought, how he'd switched from being warm and kind and friendly to suddenly cold—as if a shutter had come down. What had she said? Josh? Her mother? Something else?

Just because she'd told him her life story with hardly any prompting, it didn't mean he wanted to tell her *his*. She was supposed to be keeping her distance, anyway. And he'd probably had time to think about that kiss and regret it—that was, if he'd thought anything of it in the first place.

'See you later,' she muttered, and fled back to her own consulting room.

Alex sat staring out of the window. He really ought to go and see Jan. He was the senior partner at the practice and he'd already gone through something like it himself. He knew what it felt like so he was in the best position to help. But what was worse, he wondered, losing an unborn child to a virus, or losing an equally wanted baby to cot death?

Bethany hadn't been planned—he and Vivi had got carried away one summer afternoon—but she'd definitely been wanted. He'd gone to every single antenatal appointment with Vivi and had actually cried at the ultrasound scan when he'd seen the first picture of their baby in his wife-to-be's womb. He'd wanted to know the bond between a parent and child, the bond he'd never quite had with his own parents. He'd cut down his hours at the surgery after her birth, done his fair share of changing nappies and bathing and getting up in the night to feed the baby and soothe her when she'd had colic. He'd deliberately made the opposite choice to his mother and put his child first—until he'd gone to that damned conference.

And Vivi had phoned him with the news…

He shook himself. No. It was too easy to slide back into the grief he'd felt then, the grief that could still overwhelm him when he thought of the loss of his nine-month-old daughter. He still couldn't bear to think about what had happened next, the way Vivi had turned as cold as his mother towards him and then committed the ultimate betrayal of their marriage.

He tried to shake it off, reminding himself that his patients needed him. But it was with a heavy heart that he buzzed Lorraine to send through his first patient.

Life without Josh. It was unthinkable. There were days when Tina could literally bang her head against the wall and howl—days when Josh couldn't sit still for more than two seconds, spilled things everywhere, lost things, marched round and round her in a circle and blanked her every time she asked him something, days when she craved just five consecutive minutes of peace—but she never, ever stopped wanting him or loving him. Imagining life without him was like looking over a precipice and knowing you were going to fall straight over the edge to the bottom. So how Jan Bailey must be feeling… She shuddered.

It was worse, that morning, with three concerned mothers bringing their children in with slapped cheek. She'd had to push Jan to the back of her mind—in any case, she respected the rules of patient confidentiality so she couldn't breathe a word about what had happened to Jan.

'The rash can last up to two weeks,' she told Annie Howes, the mother of her first small patient.

'Two weeks? But…but Mrs Knight said it only lasted four days!'

Mrs Knight was the secretary at Ellingthorpe Primary. Tina knew most of the mothers in the village deferred to her as the fount of all knowledge for childhood illnesses because Mrs Knight had seen half of them through their own schooldays there and had come across just about every sort of rash over the years.

'Four days is for the milder cases,' Tina said. 'If it's just on their face, arms and legs, it'll go quickly. Can I see your tummy, Jordan?'

The little boy obligingly lifted his T-shirt to show Tina the lacy rash typical of slapped cheek over his stomach.

'Sorry, Annie. I'd put money on this one lasting two weeks.'

'But two *weeks*…' Annie made a face. 'It'll drive us both mad.'

'I know the rash is itchy, so tell him to press rather than scratch his skin,' Tina said. 'If you dab a bit of calamine lotion on it and give him tepid baths with a handful of bicarbonate of soda thrown in, it'll help with the itch. Give him paracetamol if he's got a temperature.' She smiled. 'The good news is, once the rash comes out they're not infectious any more—just the three weeks beforehand.'

'You know the school rules,' Annie said gloomily. 'He has to stay at home until the spots have gone, even though Jordan's fine in himself. He's bored and desperate to go back to school—there's the year two school trip next week and he doesn't want to miss it.'

'He should be fine for that. If he's still got a slight rash, talk it over with the school,' Tina advised. 'In the meantime, stock up on games, jigsaws and stories. Oh, and the occasional video to give *you* some sanity!'

'Thanks, Tina.' Annie smiled at her. 'How's your Josh settling in?'

'Getting there,' Tina responded, returning the smile. She was still touched by the way the other mothers at Ellingthorpe Primary had simply accepted Josh for what he was, rather than ostracising him for being a disruptive, naughty child. He'd even had invitations to birthday parties, though she'd had to decline all those with over ten guests expected—Josh simply couldn't cope in a bigger group and she didn't intend to set him up to fail.

'See you later. Come on, Jordan.' Annie looked at the pile of Lego on the floor. 'We'd better tidy this up before we go.'

'Don't worry. I'll sort it out,' Tina said. From years of practice, she could tidy up the box in ten seconds flat.

The rest of the morning flew by, and soon it was time for Tina to pick Josh up from school. While Josh ate his sandwiches, Tina rang her mother and asked if Shirley could look after Josh for an hour that afternoon. Shirley jumped at the chance. Though Tina rarely asked—knowing how difficult Josh could be on a bad day, and not wanting him to outstay his welcome—she knew that Shirley would be as delighted to see her grandson as Josh would be to spend some time with his grandmother.

So unlike Rod's parents.

But what you never had, you never missed. Josh wouldn't suffer from not being loved enough—Tina knew her parents had love enough for two sets of grandparents.

She dropped Josh off with the promise of a burger and chips for tea, then headed for the Baileys' cottage.

Warwick Bailey opened the door at her ring. 'Hello, Tina. Thanks for coming.'

'Warwick, I'm so, so sorry. I wish I…' Tina stumbled to a halt.

He shrugged. 'Nothing anyone could do. Come on in.'

Jan, the pallor of her skin and the blotchy tracks of tears showing her devastation, was sitting on the sofa.

'Don't get up,' Tina said immediately, sitting down beside her and giving her a hug. 'Dr Bowen told me the news this morning, and I wanted to see you for myself— tell you how sorry I am.'

'My baby,' Jan said softly, and a hopeless tear slid down her face.

There was nothing Tina could say. This had been Jan's last attempt at IVF, and there was no guarantee she'd conceive again even if she and her husband did manage to scrape the money together for another try. She simply held Jan close and let her sob on her shoulder.

When Jan had calmed down, Tina pulled back gently and squeezed Jan's hand. 'You know my home number. If you need to talk to me, any time of day or night, I'm there, OK?' It wasn't strictly protocol and she'd never have done that in London, but Ellingthorpe was a very close community. Tina had grown up there, so her patients were more than just medical cases, they were her neighbours and her friends. Jan needed all the support she could get right now, and Tina wasn't going to let her friend down.

'Thanks.'

'And I brought you these.' Tina fished in her bag for a large box of Belgian chocolate seashells. 'I know it doesn't even begin to compensate, but these got me through a lot when Rod died.'

'Bless you, Tina.'

'Hey. It's what friends are for. And I meant what I said. I haven't been in your situation, but I've been somewhere near it. I know pretty much how you must be feeling—so if you need me, call me.'

She hugged Warwick briefly on her way out and headed to pick up her son. It was hard to say which covered Josh more—his broad smile or half the contents of her parents' garden.

'I don't know if I dare ask,' Tina said, hands on hips as she grinned back.

'We made a worm farm,' Josh said gleefully. 'Me and Nanny put soil and sand in the jar in layers, and me and Grandad did a worm dance.'

Tina glanced at her father, seeking explanations. 'A worm dance?'

'For once, it hasn't been raining. So we had to kid the worms that it had—we watered the grass and danced on it, so they'd feel the vibrations.'

'We got three worms!' Josh crowed. 'They'll mix the sand and the soil when they eat it, and then it comes out the other end so we can see where they go.'

Tina was surprised he hadn't come out with the b-word. Like most children of his age, Josh found the word 'bottom' hysterically funny.

'And this worm farm's going to live in my kitchen, is it?'

John Lawson chuckled. 'Tina, my love, it's not as if you're that house-proud.'

Tina knew he wasn't criticising, but she still squirmed and changed the subject. 'Has Josh been OK?'

'Stop fussing, love. He's been an angel,' Shirley said.

Tina doubted that, but loved her parents the more for saying it. She knew how easily children with ADHD could end up with low self-esteem, their behaviour constantly criticised. 'Well, angel, we'd best take your worms for a burger,' she said.

Josh was still full of worm talk when they got home. He told Denise the hairdresser everything he knew about worms while she was rescuing Tina's purple streaks. All through his bath, he made up songs about worms. And Tina was just changing his sheets from where he'd left a wet towel lying on the bottom sheet, ready for him to go to bed, when she heard the doorbell ring. Before she had a chance to answer it, Josh had flung the door open, regardless of his pyjamas, invited the man on the doorstep inside and was haranguing him about worms.

'They're 'maphrodites, you know,' he said importantly. 'That means they're mummies *and* daddies at the same time. And the biggest worm in the world's nearly twice as tall as me!'

'OK, Josh, that's enough,' Tina said, hurrying downstairs. 'And remember, you're supposed to wait for me before you open the door.'

'But Mum-*mee*,' Josh began.

'I wonder if your worms have made any trails yet,' she said, and Josh took the bait, dashing off to the kitchen at top speed to inspect the jar.

'Sorry about that,' Tina said, smiling awkwardly at Alex. 'Come in.'

'I take it the blur was Josh?'

'Uh-huh. What can I do for you?'

Before he could answer, there was a crash and a wail.

Tina ran to the kitchen. The jar containing the worm farm was in pieces, the black paper covering the jar was ripped, soil and sand were everywhere, and three fat wriggly worms were making a bid for escape.

'My *farm*!' Josh howled.

'We'll make a new one tomorrow,' Tina promised. 'Stand still while I clear this up—I don't want you standing on any glass and cutting your feet—and we'll let these worms have a play in our garden tonight, OK?'

'I've got a really big jar you can have,' a voice came from the doorway. 'I'll give it to your mum at the surgery tomorrow.'

'But we have to do a worm dance to get the worms.'

'I'm a champion worm-dancer,' Alex said.

This was her *boss* talking? Tina thought in amazement. The man who'd been so cool with her this morning. The man who'd held her close, comforting her, last night. The man who'd kissed her—a soft and gentle kiss, but one that had promised so much more. The man who'd suddenly turned her life upside down and she wasn't sure how or why or what she was going to do next.

'Will you do a worm dance with me tomorrow?'

Before Tina could explain to Josh that he couldn't make demands on other people's time, Alex had agreed.

'You could come to tea,' Josh said. 'We could do our worm dance while Mummy makes tea. She can cook us noodles.'

'That'd be lovely,' Alex said. 'Thank you.'

'Come when the big hand's at the top and the little hand's on the six,' Josh informed him. 'That's when we have our tea.'

'It's a date,' Alex said.

Tina, stunned by the speed at which her boss and her son had arranged things without her, turned her attention to sweeping up the broken glass, sand and soil. She rescued the worms and put them outside, and by the time she got back Josh and Alex were both drinking milk from vividly coloured plastic beakers, and there was one set out for her as well, with a packet of chocolate biscuits in the middle of the table.

'Guess I'm superfluous,' she said.

'What's soo-pershulus?' Josh asked, stumbling over the word.

'Complicated,' Tina said, knowing Josh's delaying tactics of old and not wanting to get into a discussion. 'And you have to be in bed in five minutes as it's school tomorrow.'

'But I want to talk to Alex!'

'Dr Bowen,' Tina corrected.

'He said I could call him Alex. He's my friend.'

Tina, recognising the mutinous cast to Josh's bottom lip, gave in. 'Ten minutes.'

It was more like twenty, but when Josh was finally in bed she came back downstairs to face Alex. 'Sorry about the milk and biscuits.'

'I enjoyed it.'

'So—er—what did you want to see me about?'

'There's something different about you,' he said, his eyes narrowing.

'No purple,' Tina said, ruffling the tips of her fringe with her fingers.

Alex wished she hadn't done that. It made him really, really want to touch her.

Do it, the imp pressed, and he reached out and slid his hands through her hair. It was soft and warm and silky and almost curled round his fingers in a caress. Beautiful hair. He wanted to breathe in its scent, rub his cheek against it and then slide his mouth down to hers and…

And she was looking at him in utter shock.

'A quick purple-check, just in case any was still on the loose,' he said swiftly, snatching his hands away. 'But you pass inspection, oh, sober Dr Lawson.'

'I'm not going to live that down, am I?' she asked wryly.

'Nope,' he agreed, relieved that he'd got away with it. This time. He told the imp to shut up and stop leading him into temptation, and the imp went into sulk mode.

His common sense did a victory dance and reminded him he'd already gone too far, coming here tonight. He should have waited, talked to her at work tomorrow. Tina wasn't looking for another relationship. She was still grieving for Rod, and she'd always put Josh's needs before her own.

What about the kiss? the imp retorted, stung out of its sulk. *You haven't stopped thinking of it all day—the way her lips softened beneath yours, the way her body responded to you. And how it feels to hold her.*

It'll all end in tears, his common sense pronounced lugubriously.

Yeah, yeah. We'll deal with that when the time comes, the imp said. *Do you want to be with the woman or not?*

Alex made an effort to pull away from the battle inside his head. OK, he hadn't been able to stay away from Tina. But now he needed to convince her that his excuse for coming to see her had been a valid one. 'I came across some research today and thought you might find it useful.' He fished in the back pocket of his chinos and pulled out some web page printouts. 'It's an exercise programme which apparently has good results for kids with ADHD and Asperger's—something to do with movement encouraging the development of synapses within the brain. There's a teacher near here, apparently.'

'Thanks.' Tina took the papers from him. 'But I hope you haven't come out of your way tonight. You could have given these to me at the surgery tomorrow.'

Exactly, his common sense said smugly.

But you wouldn't have seen her like this, the imp countered, *the way she is at home: all soft and warm and relaxed instead of the dedicated yet caring professional.*

Alex realised that she was waiting. He needed a better excuse—and fast. 'I wanted to talk to you about Jan Bailey as well,' he said. 'I called round but she was sleeping and I didn't want to disturb her. Did you have a chance to see her?'

Tina nodded. 'She's very low, but that's hardly surprising. I've told her to ring me any time she wants to talk to me, and I'm going to keep an eye on her. And I thought about having a chat with her consultant, see if there's anything they can do for her—another shot at IVF perhaps. When she's ready for it, of course.' She paused. 'Don't feel you have to do the worm farm. Josh'll have forgotten about it by tomorrow.'

'You should never break promises to children.' At her glare, he added, 'I wasn't presuming to tell you what to do—just that I don't make promises I can't keep.'

'Sorry.' Tina bit her lip.

'It's OK. You probably get enough people telling you what to do with Josh—how you mustn't let him eat this or that, and you have to watch his sugar levels and don't let him have sugary drinks or chocolate.'

She stared at him with obvious surprise. 'How do you know?'

'I had a couple of children with ADHD in my last practice. I think the well-meaning comments of people who've been misled by the media into thinking that special diets cure ADHD did more to bring the parents down than the constant activity of their kids.'

'You can say that again,' she said grimly. 'Less than five per cent are affected by colours and E-numbers.' She stopped herself with an effort. 'Sorry. I'll get off my soap-box now.'

'Don't worry about it. The other thing I meant to ask,' Alex continued easily, 'was about the stones in your living room.'

'Dinosaur bones or pirate's treasure, depending on what mood Josh is in.' She sighed. 'I've been trying to wean him off them. He's banned from collecting stones at school, since the day he picked up half a dozen rocks, stuffed them in his shoe-bag, then forgot about them and swung the bag at one of his friends in the cloakroom.'

Alex smiled in sympathy. 'Sounds like the sort of thing Denzil'd do—an Asperger's syndrome patient at my old practice,' he explained. 'But if Josh is really interested in rocks, there's a unit he'd love at the craft barns just down the road in Follingford. They do rock samples at pocket-money prices—fossils, too.'

'That might be good in his reward programme,' Tina said thoughtfully. 'Five stars in a day equals one dinosaur sticker; five dinosaur stickers equals one rock or fossil. Thanks. I'll take him there one afternoon.'

'I'd…better let you get on,' Alex said. What he really wanted to do was pull her into his arms and kiss her again—kiss her senseless—but he had just enough control to stop himself. He had to take it slowly with Tina, move their relationship forward on her terms.

Not that he should be thinking of a relationship with her anyway. He'd thought that Vivi had been the opposite of his mother, warm and loving and caring, and look how that had turned out. Just because Tina adored her son and was close to her own parents, it didn't mean she'd have that same love to give to anyone else.

Or that he was capable of inspiring love—real love—in anyone. Wasn't that maybe what the real problem had been with Vivi and his mother? He wasn't lovable enough.

He pushed the thought away. 'I'll see you tomorrow morning.'

'And, Josh, tomorrow evening… If you don't mind chicken stir-fry and noodles, then you're welcome to stay for supper.'

She's only being nice. She doesn't mean it. Say no. Make an excuse. Be polite, be nice, but stay out of her way, his common sense warned him.

At that, the imp lost patience, fought a brief and very dirty battle with Alex's common sense and regained control of Alex's mouth. 'Great. I love Chinese food. And I'll bring the wine.'

CHAPTER FIVE

YOU'RE completely crazy, Tina Lawson. Why on earth did you invite him for tea?

I didn't. Josh did.

But you seconded the invitation. He couldn't exactly say no after that, could he?

Of course he could.

Yeah, right. You really fancy him, don't you?

No, I do not. It was just…being neighbourly. Colleaguely.

There isn't such a word as 'colleaguely'.

Oh, shut up.

'If talking to yourself is the first stage of madness, I hate to think what the second is,' Tina said out loud.

'I could give you a few suggestions,' a voice said in her ear, and Tina shrieked.

'Lorraine! I didn't hear you creep up on me.'

'I didn't creep, Tina. You're away with the fairies this morning,' the practice receptionist said with a grin. 'Here. One disgusting green tea with lemon.'

'Thanks. And it's not disgusting, it's good for you,' Tina said primly.

'It looks like one of the specimens old Jared Collier used to bring in,' Lorraine teased back. 'Rather you than me! Oh, and one of the drug reps brought in something nice yesterday afternoon.' She put a plate of thin straw-coloured biscuits on Tina's desk. 'They're a bit on the moreish side, so keep them away from Alex. You know

60

what a sweet tooth he's got—he's already eaten twice his fair share.'

Alex. This was ridiculous. Surely she could hear his *name* without going into a tizzy? 'Thanks. I'll remember that.' She took a bite of the biscuit. 'Mmm, he's got a point. These are gorgeous.' Shortbread flavoured with lemon zest, and so melt-in-the-mouth that you could easily eat a plateful without noticing. 'Thanks.'

'Pleasure. See you later.'

Tina smiled and sipped her tea, put the biscuits in her top drawer to stop her eating them all at once, then flicked through her computer notes to check the background of her next patient before buzzing him in.

'Good morning, Mr Pearmain. How are you feeling today?'

'Not so good,' the elderly man began, then a hacking cough covered the rest of his words. He brought a handkerchief to his mouth and spat into it. Tina could see reddish-brown stains on the crumpled white cloth. Blood. Not a good sign.

'Would you like some water?' she asked when he'd finished coughing.

'No, lass, I'll be fine.' He bit his lip. 'Thing is, my daughter sent me. I didn't want to come—nothing you can do for an old man like me who's smoked all his life, is there?'

Tina caught the undercurrent: he hadn't wanted to come because he thought he knew what was wrong. And he was convinced that what he had was fatal. Cancer.

'It depends what's wrong with you,' she said. 'How long have you been coughing like this?'

'A few weeks. I know I ought to give up the fags, but— see, I can't. They're all I've got since the wife died. Except my Tracy.'

Sensing that there was more, Tina nodded. 'Your Tracy?'

'She's a good girl, my Tracy. But that husband of hers... He thinks she spends too much time with me and not enough with her own family, even though the kids are never there half the time. You know what teenagers are. Want to be off with their mates, not hanging around with a boring old man.' Mr Pearmain shrugged. 'I don't think much of *him* either, but she loves him. I don't want him to divorce her because of me, and then she'll end up hating me for it.'

Tina made a mental note about social support. 'Maybe Tracy can persuade him to compromise.' She paused. 'Is that the first time you've coughed up blood, just now?'

Mr Pearmain shook his head. 'Been like that since the cough started. A few weeks now.'

'Apart from your cough, how have you been feeling?'

'A bit breathless, but I know that's the fags. I've lost a bit of weight but I just don't fancy food much at the moment. And I'm just tired because I'm an old man. I'm seventy-nine.' He swallowed. 'It's cancer, isn't it, Doctor?'

'I couldn't tell you without sending you for an X-ray. But coughing up blood doesn't always mean cancer.' The notes on the screen didn't go back far enough to tell her his childhood medical history, but his other symptoms nagged at her. Loss of weight, loss of appetite, tiredness, breathlessness. TB was more likely to be found in London than in rural Norfolk, but if he'd had it as a child... 'Have you ever had any problems with your lungs before?'

'A bit of weakness, but, then, I've smoked ever since I was a little 'un. And I remember my old mum saying I had something when I was little.'

The blood she'd seen had been bright red and frothy,

known as haemoptysis; it was usually a symptom of cancer or TB. If the 'something' during his childhood had been infection by Mycobacterium tuberculosis, this could be post-primary TB. 'When you cough, do you always bring something up?'

'Most times.'

'What does it look like?'

'Yellowish, sometimes with a bit of blood in it.'

'Any pains in your chest?'

He nodded.

'I'd just like to listen to your chest, Mr Pearmain—would you mind unbuttoning your shirt for me, please?'

Just as she'd suspected, there were signs of pleural effusion—fluid in the lungs—plus diminished breathing sounds and a stony, dull percussion note. TB also produced cavities in the lungs, so she needed to act on her suspicions now. 'I'm going to send you to Melbury General for some more tests,' she said as her patient restored order to his clothing. 'I'm sending you for a chest X-ray and I'd also like you to give me a sample of sputum—the stuff you cough up—so they can test it at the lab.' If her suspicions were right, the lab could do a rapid staining test that took two days; in less severe cases the germ had to be grown in the lab and it could take a couple of months until they had a result.

'So is it cancer?'

'I need to see the X-ray first but, given your other symptoms, I think it's probably TB.'

'TB? Consumption, you mean?' He frowned. 'But—that died out years ago, didn't it?'

'Unfortunately not—it's the commonest infectious disease in the world, and there are still around seven thousand cases a year in the UK. But if it is TB, we can help you get better. You'll need to be isolated while you're infectious, and you'll have a lot of tablets to take for the next six months, but it can be cured as long as you take all your tablets.' She crossed her fingers that he wasn't in the ten per cent of drug-resistant cases, which would mean a slightly longer course of different antibiotics. 'We'll need to talk to everyone you've been in contact with, so they can have a skin test—it's called a heaf test, and it's just a little prick in the forearm. If a lump comes up, it's positive, and we'll send them for a chest X-ray to check it out.' And as TB was a notifiable disease, she also needed to fill in a report form and pass on her suspicions to the consultant in communicable disease control at Melbury General.

'So I could have given this to my Tracy?'

'Not necessarily,' she said. 'It's only if you have what's called "open TB"—that means you're coughing up a lot of germs—and she's not been well herself or didn't have a BCG vaccination when she was younger that she might be at risk.'

'So I'm not going to die, then?'

She smiled. 'If I'm right and it's TB, as long as you finish the course of tablets—and I mean *finish* them, even if you still have some left when you're feeling better— you'll be fine.'

For the first time, he gave her a genuine smile. 'You've put my mind at ease, lass. Though TB...' He shook his head. 'I've never had a dirty home or drunk dirty milk.'

'TB's nothing to do with a dirty home, and it's nothing to be ashamed of,' Tina said. 'I know you used to get it through milk, but not when milk's been pasteurised.' Bovine TB, contracted from infected milk, was much rarer nowadays. 'TB was really common up to the 1950s, and if you had it as a child it sometimes comes back when your immune system's a bit low. Now, I'll ring through and get you an appointment with the chest clinic. Do you need me to arrange hospital transport?'

'No. My Tracy's a good girl. She'll take me. I won't tell *him*, though, or he won't let her,' Mr Pearmain added, clearly thinking of his son-in-law.

Four minutes later, Tina had arranged a chest X-ray appointment for the following Monday morning, taken a sputum sample and Mr Pearmain had left her consulting room, a little more of a spring in his step now his fears of cancer had been relieved.

At last morning surgery was over, and Tina went to pick up Josh. She hadn't actually seen Alex that morning—she'd only heard his deep voice in the corridor and seen the jar he'd left on her desk for the worm farm. But she'd been very, very aware of his presence, and cross with herself for letting his nearness distract her. When a patient was with her, it was fine, she could concentrate. But between patients, when she was writing up notes, she found her thoughts wandering down the other end of the corridor. Even chanting her mantra to remind her of the barriers between them—*Josh, work, Rod. Josh, work, Rod*—didn't have any effect.

Why couldn't the senior partner have been some stuffy, boring, middle-aged, *married* doctor? Instead, he was in his mid-thirties—only a couple of years older than she was—drop-dead gorgeous, and nice to boot.

More than nice.

He had to have a major character flaw, she decided. She just hadn't discovered it yet. Otherwise, why wasn't he married? Even if he was a workaholic and dedicated himself to his career, some woman would surely be waiting patiently for him. Maybe he was impossible to live with, demanding and impatient and grumpy in private.

Nope. Not convincing. She'd seen him outside work and he was even more irresistible. He'd charmed Josh, too. Her little boy was absolutely full of chatter about his new friend.

If only Alex hadn't kissed her...

Get a grip, she told herself. Nothing's going to happen.

But she could barely concentrate after work that afternoon, knowing that she was going to see him again. As the seconds ticked nearer and nearer to six, she found herself growing more and more nervous. Crazy. This wasn't a date. It wasn't as if Alex had suggested a relationship. He was coming to see Josh, to do a worm dance, that was all.

What about that kiss? the voice in her head asked.

Not again! It was *nothing*, she told herself firmly. It had been...just a friendly gesture. Business. It hadn't meant a thing to either of us.

Liar, the little voice taunted.

She ignored it and tried to focus on preparing the stir-fry. When the doorbell went, she jumped and nearly sliced her thumb open on the kitchen knife.

'I'll get it, Mummy!' Josh yelled, and zoomed past her to the front door. Before Tina could even collect her thoughts, Josh was ushering Alex through to the kitchen.

'Hi. I brought the wine.' He lifted a carrier bag for inspection. 'Fridge?'

'Yes, please.'

'Anything I can do to help?'

She shook her head. 'I'm fine.' A complete lie: she wasn't fine at all. Her hands were even shaking slightly.

But any potentially awkward moments were averted by Josh hopping up and down. 'Can we do our worm dance now? Please, please, please? You said...'

'And we will, if that's OK with your mum. It'll take

about ten minutes.' Alex winked at the little boy, then turned to Tina.

She nodded, not quite trusting herself to speak. This was the kind of thing that Rod would have done with his son... She reminded herself sharply that Alex wasn't trying to take Rod's place. He was simply being kind.

'I'll need some water. Oh, and some washing-up liquid.'

'Grandad didn't,' Josh said.

'But the ground's drier now. We need to make the worms think it's been raining, and then they'll come up.'

'That's what I did with Grandad. I made a puddle with the watering-can. Why do you need washing-up liquid?'

'It helps with the vibrations in the soil when you do the worm dance,' Alex said simply.

'The new jar's ready on the side,' Tina told him. 'Thanks for that.'

'Pleasure.'

'I did all the sand and soil layers,' Josh said proudly.

There was a brief flurry as Josh directed Alex to the washing-up liquid and a plastic jug. By the time Tina had finished cooking the noodles, chicken and vegetables, opened the wine Alex had brought and made Josh a drink of apple juice mixed with fizzy water, Josh was walking very carefully back into the kitchen with his prized worm farm. 'Me and Alex got five,' he said with glee.

'Let's put the jar at the back of the worktop where it won't get knocked,' Alex said.

Again, Tina had to swallow a large lump in her throat and remind herself that this was just the act of a friend. It didn't mean anything more. 'Just in time,' she said lightly. 'I was about to dish up and call you.'

Alex and Josh did more justice to the meal than Tina. She got away with it—just—by claiming she'd been put off by Josh's comparisons between the noodles and his worms. Yet all the time she was aware of how near Alex was to her. How dark his eyes were; the faint beginnings of stubble on his fair skin; the hairs on his forearms. How strong and yet gentle his hands were. All the time, she kept remembering how his mouth had felt on hers—gentle, questioning, then suddenly coaxing her lips into a response.

She was glad of the excuse to clear the table—it meant he couldn't look into her eyes and guess her thoughts.

'Alex, I can make a chicken out of a tea-towel. Want to see?'

'Ice cream first, Josh,' Tina said.

'But Mum-*mee*…'

'Ice cream first.'

Josh submitted only on pain of having a banana split and telling his banana joke six times. Then he launched into his party trick, with the rolled-up and folded tea-towel bearing a passing resemblance to an oven-ready chicken. 'I tried to make an ostrich with the bath-towel but it didn't work,' he informed Alex.

'It's still impressive. You'll have to teach me so I can show off to all my patients.'

Flushed with triumph, Josh looked at Tina. 'Can I, Mummy?'

She nodded. 'Go through to the living room and I'll bring coffee.' Safer than wine. Much, much safer. A hefty shot of caffeine and she'd be back in control and she'd stop thinking about that beautiful sensual mouth.

And there went another flying pig.

'I'll do the washing-up,' Alex offered.

'Don't worry. It'll only take me a minute.'

Coward, his eyes said—he could clearly tell an avoidance strategy when he saw one—but he submitted and let

Josh lead him into the living room. Tina lingered for as long as she dared in the kitchen, then finally joined them with a tray of coffee for Alex and herself and a beaker of milk for Josh.

They were bent over something together, visibly concentrating, and Tina felt a pang at the sight of her son's sandy mop next to Alex's dark hair. It was rare for Josh to take this much to a new acquaintance. Stop this right now, she thought, before he gets hurt.

Almost as if Alex had heard her silent plea, he looked up and smiled.

Tina's heart lurched.

No. She couldn't fall for him. For Josh's sake, they could only be friends. And not that close either—she couldn't bear to see Josh rejected again, the way Rod's parents had rejected him.

'Goody, chocolate biscuits,' Josh said and helped himself from the plate, oblivious to the undercurrents between Alex and Tina.

'Guests first, Josh,' Tina reminded him.

'Sorry.'

'It's OK,' Alex said. 'I'm still full anyway.'

'Mummy, look what Alex bought me! It's his host present.'

'Host present?'

'Because it's good manners to take your host a present,' Josh recited importantly. 'Look, he brought me a purple rock! It's called peacock ore. It's all purple and pink and blue and silver and gold.'

Tina dutifully admired the rock. 'It's very pretty.'

'And it sparkles, see?' Josh held it so it caught the light.

'Pocket-money rocks,' Alex said, as if he'd anticipated her protest. 'I was in Follingford anyway this afternoon, so I called in at the craft barns on the off-chance they might have something he'd like. I was going to get him a piece of amethyst, but then I saw this. It's from Mexico, Josh—it's also called bornite, and it's a type of copper ore.'

How did he know so much about rocks?

'The lady in the shop told me,' Alex said, and Tina flushed. Had she spoken aloud without realising it, or was her face just very readable? Either way, this was dangerous. She had to keep things on a purely professional footing between them. For her own sake, as well as Josh's.

'It's really pretty. Can we come to tea at your house tomorrow, Alex?'

'Josh, you can't invite yourself to people's houses!' Tina said, aghast.

'Why not?'

'It's rude. You have to wait to be asked.'

'And I can't cook anyway,' Alex said.

He wasn't telling the truth, Tina thought. No way would a capable man like Alex be unable to cook. Or maybe this was his way of letting Josh down gently.

Not that Josh was going to accept it. 'Everyone can cook. You can make sandwiches and we can have a picnic. I'll help you.' He warmed to his theme. 'I like cooking. I can make you a special biscuit, a spaceship biscuit, as my host present.'

'With purple icing?'

'And silver balls,' Josh confirmed.

'Then I guess it's a date.'

Hang on. He's supposed to be letting Josh down gently, Tina thought, horrified.

'And you'll bring your mum?'

'You can bring yours, too,' Josh said, before Tina could stop him.

'Sorry, champ, no can do. She died recently.'

'So she's in heaven, like my daddy,' Josh said.

'I'm sorry,' Tina muttered.

'It's OK.' Alex stood up.

It clearly wasn't OK, Tina thought. There had been a brief flash of pain on his face, deepening the lines around his eyes. Lines she wanted to reach up and smooth away. Kiss away. She wanted to—

'Hey, Josh, I have to be going now. But I'll see you soon.'

'Tomorrow?'

'If your mum's not too busy.'

Oh, thanks. Make me the big bad mummy for refusing, why don't you? Tina thought. 'Josh, it's the weekend.'

'So Alex doesn't have to work.'

'Yes, he does. He's a doctor. And you're going to the rare breeds farm with Nanny and Grandad tomorrow, remember? Which means we're having tea with them.'

'Oh, yes.' Josh's face showed how torn he was between the thought of a long-promised treat and spending time with his new friend. 'How 'bout the next day, then?'

'No.' She couldn't possibly impose on Alex's day off.

'Monday?' he asked hopefully.

'If Monday's OK with your mum, it's fine by me,' Alex said.

'Mum-*mee*, please, please, please?'

Tina sighed, knowing when she was beaten. 'Monday.'

'Goody!' Josh began skipping round the room.

'I'll see you on Monday in surgery,' Alex said as she walked to the front door with him.

For one heart-stopping moment, she thought he was going to kiss her again. He even leaned slightly towards her—but then he clearly thought better of it and pulled back. The rejection twisted in her stomach like a knife, and she almost flinched. And then she lifted her chin. She was strong. She could cope. And wasn't this what she wanted—distance? 'Monday,' she said. 'Goodnight. And thanks for being patient with Josh.'

'Any time.' He sketched a salute and strode off down her garden path.

Idiot, Tina thought as she closed the door. There never could have been any future in it. So stop dreaming about him. Nothing's going to happen.

Idiot, Alex thought as he walked back through the village. You know she's not ready to move on yet. So why are you pushing her into spending time with you?

There was a simple answer. He just couldn't help himself. Because he wanted to be with her.

CHAPTER SIX

NORMALLY, Tina delighted in weekends—whole days when she could spend time with Josh, take him to the beach and the park or off on a picnic. Sometimes her parents stepped in, taking Josh out for the day so she could blitz the housework without having to keep an extra ear out for him or worry about what he was doing when he was out of her sight.

This weekend was different.

This weekend was flat.

It took her until the middle of Sunday to work out why, and then it hit her. It was because the weekend meant two days of not seeing Alex.

Get a grip, she told herself. You've already been through this. You know why it can't possibly work. Ever.

And yet a corner of her heart was saying loudly that it didn't believe her.

Late on the Sunday evening, when Josh was in bed, she sat on the back doorstep, looking up at the stars. 'Help me, Rod,' she said. 'I love you. I always will. And I'll never do anything to hurt our son. But Alex… There's something about him. Something that draws me. I don't know what to do about it. He's my boss, and I…I want him to be more than that,' she whispered. 'Would it be so wrong, if I…?'

She stared up at the sky, not really expecting an answer to her half-formed question. And she wasn't surprised when none was forthcoming.

* * *

For Alex, too, the weekend was flat. He knew Tina had plans for Saturday, but she hadn't said why Sunday was out. And when Sunday dawned bright and breezy, the perfect weather for flying kites, he considered just dropping by and asking if she and Josh fancied joining him in the park. It would take him forty minutes at most to drive to the toy shop on the edge of Melbury and back. Josh would love a kite with a rocket on it. Or maybe they could make one together...

No. She's told you to back off, he reminded himself. And she's bound to have an excuse for tomorrow night, too. Leave her be.

And yet he couldn't get her out of his head.

On Monday morning, Tina found another sticky note on the corner of her PC when she walked into her consulting room. *See me when you get in, please. AB.*

Work? Or had he had second thoughts about this evening, and was going to make some kind but obvious excuse?

Be professional, she told herself, and went over to his room. She rapped lightly on the door.

'Come in.'

That smile, she thought, was unfair in the extreme. It changed Alex's face, took away the brooding Heathcliff look and made him so sexy that her knees went weak. If he'd crooked his index finger, she'd have thrown himself at his feet in a millisecond.

She put on her best GP's smile. 'You wanted to see me?'

'About Walter Pearmain. The lab team phoned me with the results this morning. You were right. It's TB.'

'Poor man.'

'I know you only had a casual contact with him, but

did you have the BCG vaccination when you were younger?'

She nodded. 'Though I'll take the heaf test if it'd make you happier. We need to start tracing his contacts and book them in for tests. I think we'll need to arrange some support in the home, too. He lives on his own and, although it sounds as if his daughter would make sure he takes all the tablets, there are some tensions with the son-in-law.'

'Resenting the time she spends with her ill parent? That's pretty common.'

There was an odd note in his voice and she looked at him closely. He wasn't married—he'd told her so himself. Divorced? And Alex's mother had died recently... Had his wife resented the time he'd spent with his mother during her illness?

None of your business, Tina.

'I'll have a word with the health visitor,' she said. 'And I'll arrange the first lot of liver-function tests for him— the poor man's really going to be sick of needles by the time it's all over.'

'As long as he completes the course.'

Patient compliance with antibiotics was notoriously bad—as soon as they felt better, they stopped taking the drugs, with the result that several diseases were becoming resistant to antibiotics. 'I made that clear.'

'I wasn't casting aspersions on your professionalism, Tina.'

No? *No.* It was an old problem—he'd probably made the comment in sympathy, and she was being over-sensitive. 'At least the posters in the surgery about antibiotics not working on colds seem to be getting the message through. Maybe we need to put up some others about completing courses of medicine.'

'Maybe.' He steepled his hands. He actually looked nervous, she thought. 'Tina, about tonight…'

'I'll explain to Josh that you're busy,' she said swiftly, forestalling the rejection. 'I'm afraid he needs to learn some social skills.'

'No, no—it's fine with me. I just wanted to check it was still OK with you. Though I meant it about my cooking. Does he like pizza?'

'Show me a kid who doesn't.' She smiled. 'It's a good way of sneaking vegetables into him—that and stir-fries. Though he'd live on burgers and chips if I let him.'

'I've got surgery this afternoon. Can Josh last out until half-past six?'

Come on, make an excuse. Tell him Josh won't wait for dinner. Tell him Josh needs a quiet night after the weekend's excitement. Tell him…

'That'd be lovely.' Her mouth definitely wasn't working in synch with her common sense.

'Do you know where Ellingthorpe Barns are?'

The conversions that just about everyone in the village lusted over? Of course she did! 'Yes.'

'I'm at number three.'

Way, way out of her league.

'See you later, then.' He gave her another of those killer smiles.

She was really going to have to give herself another talking-to about Alex.

'Thanks for telling me about Mr Pearmain's results.' She risked a small smile of her own, and left his room.

There were too many hours until half past six tonight, Alex thought. Way too many. And he didn't have any more good excuses to interrupt Tina's surgery, now he'd given her the news about Walter Pearmain. This was crazy. He'd already told himself that she was off limits. She was still grieving for her partner, she had to put her special-needs child first, and she was a work colleague. He could find hundreds of other good reasons why he should stay away.

But he couldn't do it.

It's her eyes, the imp said. *And that kiss. Imagine what it'd be like, kissing her properly, seeing her eyes grow all dark with passion. Carrying her to your bed. Making her yours…*

Alex shrugged the imp off and called in his first patient.

'So, how are you, Susie?' he asked the young redhead.

A tear spilled down her face. 'I… It's hopeless. I'm just miserable all the time and snapping at little Mike. So I wondered if you could give me some Prozac. Just to tide me over.'

'I'm not that keen on prescribing antidepressants,' he said. 'They'll help the symptoms, but they won't help the root cause—and you need to sort that out before you'll start to get really better.'

'It's all right, Dr Bowen. I understand.' Susie stood up and scrubbed at her face. 'Sorry for wasting your time.' She began to walk to the door.

'Hey, I didn't say I wouldn't help you. Just that I don't treat Prozac like sweeties.' He was at the door before her, and guided her back to her seat. 'You're unhappy and we need to do something about that. Prozac might not be the right answer but it doesn't mean I can't help you. How are you sleeping, Susie?'

'Not well.' She sighed. 'Every time I'm dropping off, I think of something and then I start worrying. All the bills…' Alex knew from long experience that if he waited for his patient to break the silence, he'd find out what was really wrong. 'Steve says he can't afford to pay anything towards my bills and I'll just have to manage, and I don't want to lose the house.' She covered her face with her hands. 'What'll I do if I lose the house? I don't want to live with my parents again. They're too old to cope with a little one running around. And if I get a job, I'll need a childminder and I can't afford it.' She shook her head. 'I don't want to be a benefits scrounger.'

'You're not a scrounger, Susie. That's what the laws are there for—to help people like you who've had a run of bad luck.' Starting with her husband leaving her for another woman and deciding that he was going to jettison his financial responsibilities as well. 'I can give you the number of someone who can help you sort out the legal side.'

'I can't afford a solicitor.'

'It's a free advisory service, completely confidential,' Alex reassured her, digging in his drawer and then handing her a card.

'Thanks.' She smiled ruefully. 'I'm sorry, Dr Bowen. I know you've got more important people to see than me, people who are really ill and not just moaning.'

'You've got as much right to be here as anyone else. You're not sleeping and you're feeling down, and I'm here to help.' He paused. 'Anything else you're worrying about?'

'Well, it's a bit embarrassing.'

'You don't need to be embarrassed with me. I'm your GP and I'm not going to laugh at you—and remember, everything you tell me remains completely confidential.'

She sighed. 'It's Mike. He's started wetting the bed again—and he's been dry for years. He's six, for goodness' sake!'

'It might be his way of showing you he's worried,' Alex said. 'Try to ignore it—I know it's a lot of extra work for you, but use a waterproof bottom sheet and make sure he washes well the next morning so other children can't detect the smell of urine and start teasing him. Then just give him lots of cuddles so he knows you love him. Lots of children his age still wet the bed—we don't consider it a real problem until a child's around seven. If you like, I can refer you to a special enuresis clinic for parents in Melbury—they'll reassure you and give you some good advice about things you can try with him.'

'Thank you. That'd be...' She spread her hands in a hopeless gesture, and Alex could see she was close to tears.

'It just takes a little time.' Then he remembered something. 'Susie, you're a registered childminder, aren't you?'

'Well—yes, though I haven't done it for a few years now. Steve said he didn't like other people's kids underfoot all the time.'

'But if you had an assessment and the authorities were happy to put you back on the register?'

She nodded. 'I could...but who'd want me to look after their kids?'

Alex knew exactly where she was coming from. He'd been there, after Vivi. What use was he as a doctor, when he was clearly inadequate and unlovable as a man? In the end, he'd moved away and started afresh, here in Ellingthorpe. Though Susie had family and close friends surrounding her, so she'd be better off staying put.

'Lots of people. Once you're registered again, you'll be on the list for the local childcare information service. And you could always put cards up on notice-boards—at the school, the toddler group and here at the surgery.'

Once Susie was working again, she'd have money coming in, she'd feel she was doing something important in the community instead of living off other people's handouts, and she'd get a lot more human contact than if she stayed at home brooding about what had happened with Steve. And talking, Alex knew, would be a lot more help to her in the long run than Prozac.

And having a childminder in the village with a child at Ellingthorpe Primary... Alex knew someone else that would help, too. 'I might know someone who'd appreciate your help right now—though I'll need to check it out first.' And on a day when Tina wasn't being pigheaded about accepting any help that might compromise her precious independence.

'Thanks, Dr Bowen.'

'Come back and see me in a fortnight,' he added. 'If you're still having the same problems, I'll give you something to tide you over.'

'All right.'

'You take care, now. And give the childcare information service a ring. They'll tell you where to go next—or there's one of the national associations.'

'I used to be a member. I'll get my old papers out,' she promised.

The rest of the morning flew by. Lunch was a hastily grabbed sandwich followed by his rounds, then late afternoon surgery, which overran by a good fifteen minutes. When he'd seen his last patient, he was about to ring the local pizza delivery company to arrange the evening's dinner when his phone rang. He picked up the receiver with resignation. 'Dr Bowen.'

At a quarter past six, as Tina and Josh were walking up the hill to Alex's house, her mobile phone rang.

'Tina? I'm sorry, I know it's late notice, but I can't make tonight. I've just been called out—it might only take a few minutes but I might be longer. I didn't want to mess you about.'

'No problem,' she said carefully. Though it *was* a problem. Josh had been looking forward to it.

'Could we take a rain-check until tomorrow night?'

She did the sensible thing. 'We'll talk about it later. Go and see your patient.' With a sigh, she switched off her mobile and crouched down so that her face was level with her son's. 'Josh, you know Alex is a doctor, like me?'

'Ye-es.'

'Sometimes people need his help, so he can't do things he planned. A patient's just called him, and he's going to be a long while, so we'll have to have pizza with him another night.'

'But Mummy, I made him a special biscuit!'

'I'll give it to him tomorrow at surgery,' Tina promised. 'I know you're disappointed, darling.' And, if she dared to admit it to herself, so was she. 'We can still have pizza. Or we could go to the drive-through burger place.'

'I can have chips?'

She nodded.

'And a strawberry milkshake?'

She nodded again.

'And I can stay up late?' he tested.

She grinned. 'No, to that one!'

'Oh, Mum-*mee*,' Josh wheedled.

'Burger, bath, bed.'

'And story?'

'And story,' she confirmed, kissing the tip of his nose. 'Come on, gorgeous. Let's go get some tea.'

Later that evening, when Josh was asleep and Tina was curled up in a chair, listening to some music, the door-bell rang.

Who'd visit her this late at night? Not her parents—they'd always ring first anyway. Hadn't there been something in the Neighbourhood Watch newsletter about bogus callers? She couldn't remember, but she wasn't taking any chances. She slipped the chain onto the door before opening it a crack to check who was there.

'Can I come in?' Alex asked.

He was the last person she'd been expecting. And her heart turned traitor, speeding up in welcome.

'I know it's late, and I'm sorry about that. I just wanted a quick chat about a couple of things—and to apologise again about tonight.'

She fiddled with the chain and opened the door properly. 'Would you like a coffee?'

'I could murder one,' he said, the sentiment clearly heartfelt.

'Milk, two sugars, isn't it?' She didn't make any comment about the sugar, but her face must have given her away.

'We're all allowed at least one bad habit,' he said with a grin. 'I like my coffee sweet.'

She wasn't going to let herself think what her own bad habit might be. If she wasn't careful, it might turn out to be Alex himself. 'How's your patient?'

He followed her into the narrow galley kitchen. 'Suspected MI.' A myocardial infarction, or heart attack, needed specialist treatment—no doubt he'd called an ambulance. His next words confirmed it. 'She's in Coronary Care at Melbury General—I followed the ambulance in to help with the handover. Her husband was pretty confused and upset about what happened—it was all so fast, he didn't know what was going on. I got in touch with the children for him, but I couldn't just leave him there on his own while he waited for them to arrive.'

'Of course not.' She looked at him. 'Have you eaten tonight?'

'No,' he admitted. 'I didn't have time.'

No surprises there. Half the doctors she knew didn't eat properly. They ate on the run, and if they had to miss a meal they'd grab a chocolate bar instead—despite the fact they ought to know better. 'Do you like eggs?'

'Tina, I don't expect you to cook for me.'

'An omelette'll take me five minutes, if that.'

'Tina…'

She rolled her eyes. 'Don't be so stubborn. If you want to make yourself useful, you can get the salad out of the fridge and fix the coffee.'

Four minutes later, Alex was sitting at the scrubbed pine kitchen table, eating a fluffy cheese and ham omelette and salad, and they each had a steaming mug of coffee.

'This is good. Thanks.'

'Pleasure.' And it was a pleasure, watching him eat. It gave her an excuse to look at that beautiful mouth, those strong yet sensitive-looking hands. Though that was dangerous: it led her thoughts down a forbidden path. An extremely forbidden path.

'I take it Josh is in bed?'

'And, for once, asleep,' she confirmed.

'I brought him this,' Alex said when he'd finished his meal, fishing in his pocket then giving her a small square package wrapped in purple tissue paper. 'It's an old magnifying glass I had knocking around at home. I thought he might like it for looking at his rocks—and to make up a bit for tonight.'

'You don't have to give him presents.'

'I wanted to,' Alex said.

Her face set, and he sighed inwardly, guessing what the

problem was. 'Tina, I'm not trying to push you. I'm not trying to take Rod's place and muscle in on Josh.'

'Aren't you?'

'No. I...' He raked a hand through his hair. 'I'm not used to saying things like this and it's bound to come out wrong.'

Stop messing about, the imp chided. *Tell her you like her.*

'I like you.'

And the rest of it, the imp prompted.

He couldn't.

Well, if you won't... The imp flexed its muscles and took control of Alex's mouth. 'No, I more than like you. You blow my mind.'

And you've just blown it completely, his common sense said with a sigh. *Meaning I have to sort out this mess.* It whacked the imp in the middle of its stomach and took control. 'But I know you're not over Rod, and you've got Josh to think of. So I'd like to be friends with you.'

'*Just* friends?'

'If it turns into something else, that's fine by me.'

More than fine, the imp said, recovering from the blow and retaliating with a rather lower one to Alex's common sense. *Tell her. Now. Touch her. Make her understand.*

Alex took Tina's hand and lifted it to his mouth. 'I'm...happy...to...wait...' he punctuated each word by kissing the tip of her thumb and each finger in turn, then drew the tip of her little finger into his mouth, sucking briefly before releasing it '...until you're ready.'

That's way too fast! His common sense went into panic mode and biffed the imp on the nose to regain control of Alex's mouth. 'But we can just be friends, if that's what you want.'

Now it was Tina's turn to have trouble finding the right words. 'I…I don't know what to say.'

He lifted his mug of coffee. 'How about, ''To friend-ship''?'

She stared at him for a long, long moment. 'To friend-ship,' she said finally.

'Good.' He moved on briskly before she had a chance to backtrack. 'Next thing.'

She looked wary. 'What?'

'I'd like you to consider doing a clinic one afternoon a week. A well-woman clinic.'

She shook her head. 'I can't. Josh.'

'That's the next thing I wanted to discuss. There's half-term coming up in a couple of weeks—I know you've booked it off as holiday, but what about the end of term? And what about the summer?'

'I'll sort it out,' she muttered.

'What if I knew of a very good childminder?'

She laughed mirthlessly. 'They're like gold dust, you know that. They're snapped up as soon as they're avail-able and their waiting lists run into months.'

'The one I'm thinking of hasn't worked in a while, but she's going to get herself registered again. I could put you in touch with her—though obviously she's not going to tell people she's available until she's registered.'

'Of course.'

'So this gives you a chance to jump the queue. You might know her, actually. Susie Dennis. She's got a little boy who's six.'

'Susie Dennis…' She thought for a moment. 'Did she used to be Susie Barton?'

Alex nodded.

'Then, yes, I know her. She was at school with me—a couple of years below me.'

'I've no idea how much experience she has with special needs,' Alex warned.

'Only one way to find out. I'll give her a ring, if you give me her number. She could meet Josh, see how they get on together—and how he gets on with her little boy.'

'Good. That's settled, then.' He finished his coffee. 'Thanks for dinner. That's two I owe you.'

'You don't owe me anything.'

'Pizza, tomorrow night. Six o'clock.'

Tina shook her head. 'I take Josh swimming on Tuesdays.'

He didn't dare ask if he could join them. For one, he didn't want her to think he was pushing her; and for another, the idea of seeing Tina in Lycra was enough to raise his blood pressure. The reality would probably blow it sky-high. 'Wednesday?'

'Wednesday.'

'Deal. Where's your dishcloth?'

'Why?'

'I'm not leaving you with the washing-up.'

'I'll do it later.'

'You wouldn't have to do it at all if it wasn't for me,' he protested. Washing-up wasn't on his list of favourite things, but he'd jump at any excuse to stay near her.

'Doesn't matter. And before you go, I've got something for you.'

A kiss!

Shut up, you fool, he told the imp. Of course it wasn't a kiss. You've agreed to be just friends, remember?

Tina handed him a shiny foil package. 'With the compliments of the mini-chef.'

'The spaceship biscuit?' he guessed.

Her smile broadened. 'Just close your eyes when you eat it. It's edible, but it's a bit…bright.'

'Purple?'

'What else?'

Alex returned the smile. 'Tell him thanks for me.'

Kiss her goodnight, the imp pleaded. *Properly.*

His common sense was implacable. *Not yet. Too soon.*

But shaking her hand was too formal. In the end, he took the coward's way out and sketched a salute. 'See you tomorrow, then. I'll see myself out.'

CHAPTER SEVEN

You blow my mind.

With that and what Alex had done to her fingertips, that was an end to her getting any sleep tonight.

Tina stacked the washing-up on the draining board, promising herself to do it with the breakfast things, then made herself a mug of hot milk in the forlorn hope that it might help her sleep. She knew that warm milk contained an amino acid—tryptophan—which helped the body produce serotonin, a brain chemical that induced a sense of calm. She just hoped that it worked for her. But after what Alex had said…she doubted it.

You blow my mind.

So much for calm. Even thinking of what he'd said more than ruffled her composure. This was crazy. He hadn't made any promises. He'd even said he wasn't trying to take Rod's place. He'd agreed to be just friends.

You blow my mind.

If she wasn't such a coward, she'd have told him she felt the same. But she was a sensible doctor who wasn't going to take any risks.

And a wimp, her heart added in a disgruntled postscript.

Tina did manage to sleep, in the end—though her dreams were filled with Alex. When she woke, she was actually shaking, and she blushed when she thought about what they'd done together in fantasyland. The way he'd kissed her, touched her, aroused her, brought her closer to the edge until she'd been begging for release…

And when she actually saw him, the next morning, she couldn't help flushing to the roots of her hair. She only hoped he couldn't read her mind.

'Tell Josh the biscuit was lovely,' he said. His eyes added another message that she was too scared to read.

'He says thanks for the magnifying glass.' Tina handed him an envelope. 'He made you a card before breakfast.'

'Thanks.' His fingers touched hers for an instant and she felt as if flame had travelled the length of her arm. What was it about him that affected her like this? Even with Rod, it hadn't been quite like this.

It's *obvious* why. You've been on your own for over a year. You're a healthy young woman with normal urges that haven't been fulfilled for a while. It's just a biological thing. Hormonal, even. Get a grip, she told herself crossly.

'See you later. Surgery,' she babbled, and fled to the safety of her consulting room.

The next morning was even stickier. How she managed to get through the usual Wednesday staff meeting without staring at Alex the whole time was beyond her. Her brain had been acting on autopilot and she had no idea what she'd contributed to the meeting—clearly she hadn't said anything completely stupid, because no one had looked at her strangely or made any comments.

She managed to concentrate on her patients in surgery—just—but she was running on pure nervous energy by the time she and Josh walked up the hill to the barn complex that evening.

Why on earth had she agreed to have dinner with him? Why hadn't she phoned him and made an excuse—said that Josh was running a temperature, her washing machine had broken and she had to wait in for the repairman, she didn't have dinner out on a day with a Y in it?

You know why, the little voice in her head taunted.

She was distracted from answering by Josh pressing the doorbell—and because he liked the sound so much he did it again. Six times.

Alex answered the door with a grin. To Tina's relief, he didn't say a word about Josh's mistreatment of his doorbell. 'Hi! Come in.'

'Wow,' Josh said as he looked round the living room. 'This is *huge*!'

And incredibly neat and tidy. Josh could wreak his hurricane effect in seconds. Alex's furniture was all antique, the rug in front of the open fire an expensive silk kelim and the plates on the Welsh dresser clearly family heirlooms. Tina couldn't bear to think how much it would all cost to replace. She went straight into panic mode. 'Remember what we agreed, Josh. Walk, don't run. And no touching.'

Alex's eyes telegraphed a mixture of understanding and reassurance. 'He's fine. Hey, Josh, I found my old train set. Fancy helping me build a track?'

'Oh, yes!' Excitement made the last word into a three-syllable fall and rise, and when Alex tipped the track into a huge pile on the floor, the little boy launched straight into building a complex track layout.

Alex handed Tina a glass of wine, saying quietly, 'Don't worry about him, he'll be fine and he can't do any damage.'

'Mmm-hmm.' She wasn't quite convinced, but by the time their pizza arrived and they'd moved into Alex's kitchen—equally large and state of the art, with granite worktops and Shaker-style units and a huge beech table in the middle—she had begun to relax. There was only Alex's nearness to unsettle her. He behaved impeccably, treating her just as a friend and colleague, but she couldn't get his words out of her head.

You blow my mind.

She couldn't do it. She really couldn't.

And yet she wanted to. She really, really wanted to. She wanted to repeat that kiss, but this time to take it further. Much further.

His fingers touched hers when he offered her the dish of garlic bread and her hands shook. He touched her again when he passed the salad dressing, and her body went up in flames. And again when he passed her a white china demitasse of espresso, and she nearly dropped it. As it was, she spilled her coffee into the saucer.

She was sure he was doing it deliberately. But all the while Alex chatted with Josh as if he were completely oblivious of the undercurrents running between them.

By the time she and Josh came to leave, Tina was a quivering, shaking mess. And then, at the door, Alex leaned over and kissed her cheek. It took a superhuman effort to stop herself reaching up to slide her hands round his neck, draw his face down to hers and kiss him properly.

Only Josh's presence stopped her.

'See you tomorrow,' she said shakily.

He knew. She could see it in his eyes. He *knew*.

Her only satisfaction was that it looked as if he was in worse torment than she was. If that were possible.

Two more days at work. Two more days of torture, having him near but not near enough. And then Saturday dawned bright and sunny. Time to escape, she thought. Blow the cobwebs out and common sense back in. 'Right. We're going to the beach,' she told Josh.

He did a war dance of delight round the kitchen which ended with half a dozen eggs mushed on the floor.

'Sorry, Mummy.' His eyes filled with tears. 'I didn't mean it. It was a accident.'

Tina didn't bother correcting his grammar, knowing that he needed a hug more. 'It's OK, sweetheart. Accidents happen. Tell you what, go and find your bucket and spade while I mop this lot up and make us a picnic.' She paid no attention when she heard him talking—Josh talked to himself all the time—but then her early warning system kicked in.

Alex.

Don't be daft. Did you hear the doorbell ring?

Alex.

You're imagining things.

'Good morning.'

She shrieked and nearly dropped the bread.

'Sorry, I didn't mean to startle you. It's a nice day and it's my turn for Saturday off, so I wondered if you and Josh would like to come out with me for the day?'

'I've got my bucket and spade all ready, Mummy,' Josh piped up. 'Mummy was going to take me to the beach. Mummy, can Alex come with us?'

A whole day in his company? It'd be bliss—and torture at the same time. He looked utterly edible in a plain black T-shirt and faded jeans that moulded themselves to his rear. This wasn't fair. Why did he have to look so—so *gorgeous*? She peeled her eyes off the view and forced her voice to sound casual. 'If he'd like to.' She didn't dare meet Alex's eyes, fiddling with the bread instead. 'I'm just making a picnic. Tuna pâté sandwiches OK with you?'

'Live dangerously,' Alex said, shocking her into meeting his eyes.

Sexy eyes. Eyes which told her he wasn't talking about

just food. She tore her gaze away before she said something stupid—something like 'kiss me'.

'If we go to Holbury-next-the-Sea, the chippie on the harbour front does the best fish and chips in the world,' he added.

She knew that. She'd grown up around here after all.

He misinterpreted her silence. 'I know a picnic's healthier, but we'll need to build our strength up if we're going to catch crabs off the harbour.'

'We're going crabbing? Yeah!' Josh punched the air in delight and started hopping round the kitchen.

'My car or yours?' Alex asked Tina.

'Mine.' If she drove, she'd be forced to concentrate on the road. Which meant she'd manage to stop herself drooling over Alex.

'Then the fish and chips and ice creams are on me.'

'Deal.' Though she was too chicken to shake on it. And, from the smile that quirked his lips when she glanced up at him, he knew it.

To her relief, Alex sat in the back with Josh. Having him sit next to her would have been too much to handle. And then she realised from the conversation floating over from the back seat that Josh was reading Alex a story from one of his magazines—a story about the seaside.

How had Alex managed to do what she couldn't—persuade her clever yet wayward son to read? Or maybe it was because he was a man. She knew that boys needed male role models when it came to reading, particularly reluctant readers like Josh. Josh the perfectionist, who, if he couldn't do it all right first time, claimed he couldn't do any of it at all. Josh, whose eyes glazed over halfway down a page. And here he was, stumbling over some of the words and taking Alex's gentle yet positive correction to heart, repeating the word properly.

She tried not to feel jealous. But Josh was *her* son.

Grow up, she told herself. It's Josh who's important. It doesn't matter who's the one to boost his confidence, as long as he's reading.

But it still made her feel jealous.

Worse, she wasn't sure who she felt more jealous of—Alex, for succeeding with Josh where she'd failed dismally, or Josh, for having Alex's undivided attention.

Finally, they arrived at Holbury and she parked in the car park next to the harbour. 'Fancy a walk first?' Alex suggested.

'Yes, but you need your sunhat on, Josh. And suncream,' Tina directed. It wasn't high summer, but he could still burn in the midday sun. She smoothed the protective coloured lotion into the little boy's skin.

And then Alex took the tube from her hands.

'He's not the only one with fair skin,' he pointed out.

To Tina's shock, he proceeded to rub suncream into the back of her neck. All her nerve-endings sang with bliss, and her body turned complete traitor. 'Thank you,' she muttered, and jammed her sunglasses and baseball cap on. She didn't want him seeing how dilated her pupils were. And why hadn't she worn a much, much looser T-shirt? A suit of armour would have been better!

'What about you?' she asked.

'If you're offering.'

He sat on the harbour wall so she could reach him more easily. Touching him was torture. Sheer, absolute torture. She rubbed suncream into the back of his neck, but it would have been so, so easy to bend down and touch her lips to his skin instead. Or slide her hands under his T-shirt to caress his broad, muscular back. Or…

Stop right there, you wanton hussy, she told herself, and put the suncream back in her beach bag.

She risked a glance at him before he put his own sunglasses on. And discovered that his eyes were so dark, they were almost black. And hot. So hot. She didn't dare let her gaze travel any further down his body—she knew already that he was as aroused as she was.

This friendship thing was going to be damned near impossible.

But she couldn't take it any further. For Josh's sake.

The silence stretched out as they walked down the long path that ran alongside the harbour channel. Alex itched to take Tina's hand but stopped himself. She had to make the first move. When she did, he'd meet her all the way, but he'd promised not to push her. He'd already gone close to the edge, putting suncream on her and then asking her to put suncream on the back of his neck. It had been hell, having her touching him so dispassionately.

Though he had a sneaking feeling that it had affected her in exactly the same way that it had affected him. Which was why she didn't trust herself to speak and why she'd pulled the peak of her baseball cap down to hide her expression.

Josh was completely oblivious to the tension and scampered on happily in front of them, swinging his bucket. He stopped every so often and hopped impatiently on the spot until the adults caught up with him.

'How did things go with Susie?' Alex asked at last.

'Fine. She isn't re-registered yet, but I'm happy that she knows what she's doing. We had a trial afternoon and Josh likes her. He gets on well with Mike, too—Mike's older and knows more about football and rockets, so there's a bit of hero-worship on Josh's part. It's going to

work out well—he'll boost Mike's confidence, and
Mike'll help calm him down.'

'That's good. So you'll do the well-woman clinic?'

'Yes.'

His hand brushed deliberately against hers. Go on, take
it, he willed.

She didn't.

But she didn't pull away either.

At last they reached the beach, and Josh spent ages collecting shells and examining them with his magnifying
glass. He went hand in hand with Alex to get ice creams
from the refreshment hut on the edge of the dunes, and
Tina had to turn away. It was too much like old times,
the way Josh and Rod had gone together to the ice-cream
kiosk on the beach. They could have been any other family on the beach.

Except they weren't a family.

She couldn't expect Alex to take Josh on as well as
her. And she wasn't going to jeopardise Josh's security.
Ever. When they got home, she'd have to find a way of
telling Alex that this friendship thing wasn't going to
work and they'd have to stay away from each other. She
busied herself making a sandcastle, digging a moat round
it. Not as deep as the hole she'd been about to fall into,
she thought ruefully.

'Josh tells me you always have a chocolate flake in
yours,' Alex told her, handing her a cornet.

'Chocolate's my bad habit.' She wished he'd take his
eyes off her mouth. And then maybe she'd stop thinking
of his. And she'd find it easier to resist the temptation to
lick the soft creamy mixture from the corner of his lips.

The moment passed when Josh finished his ice cream

well before everyone else and demanded help to fill the moat.

Once the sandcastle was completed to his satisfaction and they'd played an energetic game of ball, Alex suggested taking the small narrow-gauge train back from the beach to the harbour front.

The only thing was, the carriages were so small that she was virtually sitting on his lap. Sitting side by side, she'd be squashed against him; and sitting opposite was even more dangerous because they had to fit their legs round each other's. Even having Josh sitting on her lap didn't make the situation feel any less intimate. Her imagination was working overtime and the slight flush on Alex's cheeks told her that his was doing likewise. Was he seeing the same thing as she was—the two of them lying together, skin to skin, their legs entangled?

'I'm starving,' Josh announced suddenly.

'So you want lots of chips with your fish?' Alex asked.

'Oh, yes! Please,' Josh added, belatedly remembering his manners.

Tina ruffled his hair, silently blessing her son for defusing the tension. Alex dutifully queued up for fish and chips while Tina and Josh sat on the harbour wall.

'This should be on prescription,' Alex said when he'd taken his first mouthful of fish. 'Freshly caught and cooked fish, eaten on the harbour wall in the sunshine. Best cure for depression.'

'Speaking of depression—have you seen Jan?' Tina asked.

For a moment, she thought he was going to say something about talking shop when they were both officially off duty, but eventually he nodded. 'Yesterday afternoon. She's very low. I'm going to have a quiet word with the head about ways to get her back into school. I know it's going to be hard, having children round her—but the longer she spends on her own, brooding, the worse it's going to be.'

'Have you heard anything from the consultant?'

Alex seemed to catch her train of thought. 'He says no go. It was her third attempt, and the stats aren't in her favour. She's getting older, they didn't manage to harvest that many viable eggs last time, and he feels it isn't fair to raise her expectations when the chances are so low.'

'How about adoption? Fostering?'

'Maybe.' Alex sighed. 'But let's talk about it later. We're supposed to be having a day off.'

The 'we' almost undid her. But then Josh decided he'd had enough chips and wanted to catch crabs. Again silently blessing her son for stopping her doing something stupid, Tina joined him at the harbour's edge, having bought a line and bait and a bucket full of water from the kiosk on the quayside.

Alex turned it into a competition by buying a second set of crabbing equipment. Josh won—just—and although Tina knew Alex had done it deliberately, Josh believed he'd caught more crabs fairly and squarely. They released the tiny crabs back into the sea and celebrated with another ice cream. Another walk along the harbour, half an hour for Josh to rush about on the adventure playground, and it was time to go home.

To Tina's surprise, Josh fell asleep in the car on the way home. She caught a glimpse of him in the rear-view mirror, his head on Alex's shoulder and Alex's arm curled protectively round him, and a huge lump came into her throat. Her precious, special child… She really couldn't risk his happiness.

Which was why she had the strength to say no when

she parked outside the barns and Alex asked her in for supper.

'It's been a long day for Josh. He needs a bath and then bed,' she said.

'Well, thanks for a lovely day. See you later.' And then Alex bent and kissed her cheek.

It was completely chaste.

And it turned her knees to mush.

She had no idea how she managed to drive home at all, much less drive safely, but at last they were home. Josh spent half an hour splashing happily in the bath and talking about how wonderful his new friend Alex was. 'He's lovely, isn't he, Mummy?'

'Yes, darling.'

'I like him. Don't you?'

Please, stop asking me. 'Yes, Josh.'

'Can he come and play tomorrow?'

'He's probably busy.'

'But you could ring him and ask him.'

'Later,' she prevaricated.

Maybe she should ring him. Maybe she should give in to the bone-melting desire. Maybe she should have a casual affair with him and just get it out of her system and his.

Except she was very afraid that it wouldn't work. Because a casual affair with Alex Bowen would never, ever be enough for her.

CHAPTER EIGHT

'THE dolphin swims in the sea,' Josh read slowly. 'The— oh, look, it's a shark! He's not going to eat the dolphin, is he, Alex?'

'There's only one way to find out,' Alex said. 'Let's read the book together.'

'The fish swim in... I don't know that word. I can't do it. It's too *hard*.'

'It's a hard one because the first C sounds like an S,' Alex said. 'See if you can spell it out.'

One small determined finger worked its way along the word as Josh spelled it out, and Tina could see a small frown of concentration on his forehead. Alex was completely relaxed—whereas she was always tied up in knots when they read together. Maybe that was his secret. Being relaxed.

'Circles.'

'Well done,' Alex encouraged. 'Let's do the next page.'

Under his patient yet persistent encouragement, Josh read the whole book while Tina concentrated on making spaghetti sauce.

'Well done. Now, I've got something for you for being so clever.'

'What?'

Alex took a small box from his pocket and handed it to Josh.

'Wow, it's a shark's tooth! Look, Mummy, it's a real shark's tooth!' Josh bounced across the room to her and thrust the yellow fang into her hand. 'Look!'

Tina duly admired it, then raised an eyebrow at him. 'Is there something you want to say to Alex?'

'Oh, yes. Thank you, Alex. It's brilliant. And I love you,' Josh said, running back to Alex and flinging his arms round him.

'Hey, my pleasure.'

Thank God he hadn't said that he loved Josh, too. Tina couldn't have handled that. She busied herself fiddling with things by the cooker that didn't really need fiddling with, and left them to talk sharks.

The next day saw Tina's greatest challenge yet—the afternoon well-woman clinic. The challenge wasn't so much the patients, more that she was on tenterhooks about Josh. She was sure that Susie knew how to handle him, but what if? What if? What if?

If there's a problem, she'll ring you. You've got to loosen the apron strings and let Josh learn to be independent from you, she reminded herself. But he was so small, so young, so special…

And Susie'll take good care of him, she reassured herself. She took a sip of iced water to calm herself, then called in her first patient.

'Hello, Mrs James. How are you?'

'Fine, fine.' Though clearly she wasn't—Isobel James was twisting her fingers together in her lap and wouldn't meet Tina's eyes.

This was a well-woman clinic, so no doubt it was something Isobel considered embarrassing. 'I see from your notes that you had a smear test a couple of months ago—with perfectly normal results, I'm pleased to say—and you have two children,' Tina said, to open up the discussion.

'A girl and a boy.'

Still no eye contact. Whatever the problem was, it was

really upsetting her patient. 'Sometimes your body takes a while to get back to normal after childbirth,' Tina said gently. 'How are your periods?'

'Oh, they're back to normal.'

She sounded quite unconcerned, so it wasn't that. 'Any pain?'

She shook her head, this time looking less embarrassed. 'No.'

Not painful periods, and probably not painful intercourse either. 'So how can I help, Mrs James?'

'It's…' She shook her head. 'It's so embarrassing.'

'I'm your doctor, Mrs James. I'm here to help, and I'm not going to laugh at you. One of the reasons I'm running the well-woman clinic this afternoon is because I'm female and hopefully it'll make it less embarrassing for anyone who needs help to tell me what the problem is.'

'It's just…' Isobel flushed. 'I keep *leaking*,' she whispered.

She'd said earlier that her periods were back to normal. Which meant… 'When you cough or sneeze?' Tina asked.

Isobel looked surprised. 'How did you know?'

'Because you've had two children,' Tina said, 'and around six million women share the same problem. It's called stress incontinence, and one of the reasons it happens is because your baby's weight puts pressure on your pelvic floor.' Being overweight didn't help, but that wasn't a problem in this case because Isobel looked well within her optimum weight range. 'Were your babies particularly big?'

'The first was four kilos, the second nearly five,' Isobel said. 'I had to have a forceps delivery with my son.'

'Not surprising, then.' Tina smiled. 'How bad is it? Just a small amount, or a lot?'

'It's been getting worse,' Isobel admitted. 'I've had to

give up my exercise class. Every time I did a star jump, I leaked. I was sure everyone in the class knew, and I was so embarrassed.'

'They probably didn't—and I bet at least two others in the class had the same problem,' Tina said gently. 'The good news is, I can do something to help. Did anyone teach you how to do pelvic-floor exercises while you were pregnant?'

'The ones where you squeeze and hold, as if you're stopping yourself going to the loo?'

Tina nodded.

Isobel flushed. 'Yes, but...'

'You never got the time to do them once the baby arrived,' Tina finished wryly. 'I know. I was just as bad. But you need to start doing them now—and you need to do them every single day.' She pressed a key on her computer and printed out an information sheet. 'This gives you some ideas of what you can start doing now at home, and I can book you in with a specialist nurse who can teach you how to use weighted cones to train your pelvic-floor muscles.' She smiled. 'Although they don't do much more than the exercises your midwife taught you, they're a visible reminder to actually do the exercises—it's too easy to forget, otherwise. Do you have to do any lifting?'

'Only the children.'

'Good—lifting heavy loads puts an added strain on your muscles so it's best to avoid it if you can. You need to drink plenty of water, too.'

'But—won't that make it worse?'

Tina shook her head. 'If you're not drinking enough, your urine's too concentrated and can irritate your bladder, and that *will* make it worse. Try to steer clear of coffee and caffeinated drinks, too, as they can irritate your bladder. Drinking more will help make sure you don't suffer from constipation, which puts more strain on your pelvic floor.'

'So…I'm not going to have to wear pads?'

'They might help until you get your muscle tone back—but they're much more discreet now than the bulky old things you're probably thinking about.' Tina smiled. 'You won't need to use them for ever, if that's what you mean.'

Isobel's shoulders sagged with relief. 'I wish I'd come to see you months ago. I just… I felt I was old before my time. My grandmother was incontinent, and I couldn't bear the thought of being like that in my thirties.'

'You won't be,' Tina promised. 'But you need to start doing those exercises. For now, try doing them every time you put the kettle on or walk up the stairs—whatever you do a lot in the course of the day. It'll take a couple of months before you see an improvement, but you *will* see an improvement. I'll make you an appointment with the specialist nurse, and you can take it from there—but if you're worried about anything at any time, come and see me.' She paused. 'Anything else that's worrying you?'

'No. Just the…' Isobel's mouth twisted in distaste '…leaking.'

'Less than three months, and you'll be back doing those star jumps with everyone else,' Tina said. 'In the meantime, you could try using a vaginal tampon while you're doing sport. It'll support the neck of your bladder and help stop leaks.'

'So I can go back to my class? And I'm going to be normal again?'

'You're normal now,' Tina reminded her. 'There's another six million women out there with exactly the same problem.'

Isobel James smiled for the first time. 'Thank you. You don't know how much that means, to hear that.'

The rest of the afternoon flew by. Tina did three smear tests—making sure she warmed the speculum first—and saw two women with thrush and another with a bad case of cystitis. Her last patient of the afternoon was having trouble with the beginning of the menopause.

'Every five minutes, I'm like a tomato,' Marcia Stephens said. 'The hot flushes even wake me up at night—and I'm dripping. I have to change the sheets at least once a night. Heaven only knows what it'll be like in the middle of the summer. My Frank said I ought to come and see you and get HRT, but my sister says I can't have it because I'm taking tablets for high blood pressure and you can't do both at the same time. I just don't know what to do for the best.'

'You still need to take your diuretics,' Tina said, 'but your sister's information is a bit out of date—taking blood-pressure medication doesn't mean you can't use HRT as well. What do you know about HRT?'

'Not a lot,' Marcia admitted. 'But I read something in the paper the other week about it causing breast cancer and heart attacks.'

'There's a slightly increased risk of breast cancer and heart attacks, particularly if you use HRT for more than five years; there's also an increased risk of blood clots, leading to strokes. So you do need to think about the drawbacks as well as the benefits,' Tina agreed. 'For every ten thousand women on some form of HRT, an extra eight will have a heart attack or breast cancer, so the risks are a bit less scary than you might have read in the papers. There are some benefits, too—as well as helping with symptoms such as flushes, sweating and vaginal dryness, HRT can protect you against brittle bones and bowel cancer. Some studies say it might protect against Alzheimer's.' She paused. 'But only you can decide whether it's right for you once you've weighed up the risks. Is there any history of breast cancer, heart attacks or strokes in your family?'

'My aunt had breast cancer.' Marcia shook her head. 'Though she was an aunt by marriage, not blood.'

Tina nodded. 'As you're over 50, you're automatically on the breast-screening programme anyway—though it's less effective in women under sixty because your breast tissue's denser. And even if you have a mammogram, you still need to keep checking your breasts and come straight to us if you find anything unusual.'

'HRT makes you put weight on, doesn't it?'

'It can. Some women find it makes them feel a bit premenstrual—irritable or tearful. But we can try different types of HRT to find which one suits you best, if you decide you'd like to try it. Short term, it can really help with problems, but I definitely don't recommend staying on it long term. If you're at all worried about it, you don't have to take it—there are other things you can do to help with any really nagging symptoms of the menopause. There's an alternative to HRT called selective oestrogen receptor modulators—it imitates the good effects of oestrogen on your bone density and blood fats but doesn't increase your risk of cancer. You could consider homeopathy, too—Agnus Castara helps some women. I can't prescribe homeopathic remedies, but I can give you the name of some local registered homeopaths.'

Tina gave her an information sheet she'd printed out earlier. 'This tells you all about HRT—what it does, how it works, what it can help with and what it can't help with, as well as the side-effects and when it's not suitable for you. Have a look through this lot, and if you come back and see me again next week we can talk through any other questions you might have. I'm not going to pressure you either way. I'd rather you looked at the facts and came to your own decision.'

'I'll do that, Dr Lawson.' Marcia smiled and put the leaflet in her bag. 'Thanks.'

Tina had just turned off the computer when there was a knock at her door. She frowned. She'd seen all the patients on her list—hadn't she? 'Come in.'

Alex leaned round the door. 'Hi. How was it?'

'Fine.'

'But you're desperate to rush off to Susie's and see Josh.'

She nodded. 'I know it's pathetic.'

'No, it's understandable. You're a mum and he's special.' He smiled at her. 'I won't keep you much longer. Except…I wondered if you'd have lunch with me before surgery on Thursday.'

She shook her head. 'Sorry. Josh has lunch at home.'

'Maybe having lunch at Susie's will be a first step towards lunch at school,' he suggested.

She thought about it. Lunch with Alex. Just the two of them. Crazy. Dangerous. 'I'll ask Susie and tell you tomorrow,' her mouth said.

His smile was enough to raise her blood pressure several notches.

She left the surgery and went straight over to Susie's. Josh was reluctant to leave because he'd had such a good time, and Tina finally relaxed. She was definitely doing the right thing, giving him a little more independence. Maybe Alex had a point.

'Susie, would it be possible for him to have lunch with you on Thursday?' she asked.

'No problem.' Susie nodded. 'I'll pick him up from school, shall I?'

'Thanks, I appreciate it. I'll tell Donna Ellis so she'll expect you instead of me, and I'll pick him up from you at, say, half two?'

'That's fine.'

'Great.' She ruffled Josh's hair. 'Ready to go, gorgeous?'

Josh's lower lip protruded. 'I was playing with Mike. Can I stay a bit longer? Please?'

'Next time,' she promised.

'Bye, Donna. Bye, Mike!' Josh gave both of them a hug before he left.

'Is Alex coming over tonight?' Josh asked as they walked home.

'No.'

'Why don't you ring him?'

Because I don't trust myself with him. I must have been mad to agree to have lunch with him. 'He's busy, honey.'

'But, Mummy…'

To her relief, Josh subsided at the brief shake of her head. Right now, she didn't dare think of Alex. When she saw him with Josh, it was different—casual, just as friends. But she'd agreed to have lunch with him. Just the two of them. Was this a step forward—or the beginning of the end?

Light. Keep it light, Alex told himself on Thursday morning. Nothing fancy. Granary bread, good cheese, ham, apples.

Come off it, the imp said scornfully. *You're having lunch with Tina. Make an effort.*

And scare her off? Alex's common sense asked.

There was a brief and very dirty fight. Alex's commor

sense ended up with sticking plaster over its mouth and the imp went into overdrive, making Alex miss the turning to the supermarket so he ended up outside an exclusive deli in Melbury. A quarter of an hour later, Alex had a box filled with tiny water biscuits, a creamy ripe Brie, baby plum tomatoes, black grapes, miniature blinis, sour cream and smoked salmon. And something else that had driven the imp into an absolute frenzy...

At a quarter to twelve, he was pacing the kitchen floor.

At ten to twelve, he was sweating.

At five to twelve, he was considering ringing Tina at the surgery to call it off.

And at twelve, his doorbell rang.

He reached the door in three strides. 'Come in. Drink?'

'Something soft, please.'

He'd guessed she'd say that. Which was the only reason why he didn't have a bottle of chilled champagne waiting in the fridge. 'Elderflower cordial and fizzy water?' he suggested.

'Lovely.' She handed him a box. 'My contribution to lunch.'

He peeked inside. 'Strawberries?'

'The first English ones.' Her eyes crinkled with mischief. 'Josh and I raided my dad's greenhouse last night.'

The picture it conjured up made him smile. 'Well, thanks.' And they'd go very well with what he'd originally planned for pudding.

'Got any balsamic vinegar?'

'No.' Was she teasing him? 'Why?'

'For the strawberries. It brings out the taste,' she explained. 'Black pepper's OK, but not as effective.'

She was definitely teasing. Everyone knew fresh strawberries went best with cream. Or what he'd bought for pudding. 'Hmm. Think I'll pass on the vinegar.'

Stop making polite conversation, the imp muttered. 'Take a seat,' Alex said, ushering her into the kitchen.

She pulled out a chair as he made them both a drink. 'Wow. This is *lunch*?' she said as she saw the spread on the beechwood table. 'I was expecting a sandwich, if I was lucky.'

'Just because I can't cook, it doesn't mean I eat boring food.' He took the chair opposite her.

Take it slowly, his common sense said.

The imp went back to work with the sticking plaster, then whispered in Alex's ear.

Alex picked up a tiny blini, smeared sour cream on it and topped it with a piece of smoked salmon. 'Close your eyes and open your mouth,' he said.

Lunch had just turned into something a lot more dangerous, Tina thought. She shouldn't be doing this. And yet those dark, dark eyes challenged her. A shiver ran through her; she closed her eyes and opened her mouth and let him feed her the morsel.

Josh, work, Rod.

The mantra failed. Spectacularly. Because she in turn smeared a blini with sour cream, topped it with smoked salmon and looked him straight in the eye. 'Open your mouth,' she echoed huskily.

His eyes locked with hers as she fed him. He licked the tips of her fingers, and something began to smoulder low in her belly.

He fed her a baby plum tomato.

She did the same to him.

He held out a creamy piece of Brie for her to bite into— then deliberately ate the other half.

She fed him another blini, stroking his lower lip with her thumb.

He traced the outline of her lips with a black grape.

She moistened her lips as she fed him a piece of Brie, and his pupils expanded rapidly.

By the time they'd moved on to pudding—the sweet ripe strawberries she'd brought, plus tiny profiteroles filled with white chocolate mousse—Alex's common sense had washed its hands of the whole thing and the imp was happily in charge. So Alex pulled Tina onto his lap, fed her a profiterole, then leaned forward to lick the sweet chocolate cream from the corner of her mouth.

Tina gasped.

And he kissed her. Gently, at first, and then with increasing passion as she kissed him back. Her hands were in his hair, urging him on. His fingers pulled her sensible white shirt from the waistband of her skirt and slid upwards, revelling in the feel of her skin against his fingertips.

He stopped just at the bottom of her ribcage, and broke the kiss.

'You blow my mind,' he told her again, his voice raw with need, and she shivered.

'This isn't fair, Alex. You said just friends.'

'I meant it. Sincerely. But you do something to me, Tina, and I can't help myself.' He rubbed the tip of his nose against hers, then kissed her again. This time, she was the one to pull his shirt from the waistband of his chinos and explore his skin.

'Now who's not being fair?' he asked.

She grinned and nibbled his lower lip. 'You started it.'

'And if I didn't have surgery in half an hour, I'd continue.' Reluctantly, Alex shifted her off his lap and back to her own chair. 'I want you, Tina. I want you more than I've ever wanted anything in my life. And that scares me.'

'It scares me, too,' she whispered.

He took her hand and, keeping his gaze locked with hers, kissed the tip of her thumb and then each finger in turn. 'Tomorrow's my afternoon off.'

She swallowed hard. 'And?'

'And I'd like to have lunch with you again. Just like this. Except, tomorrow, you won't have clinic and I won't have surgery.'

Which meant that they could…

'Yes,' she said, and he kissed her again.

When he broke the kiss, they were both shaking.

'You can back out any time you please,' he told her. Though his eyes pleaded with her not to.

She didn't. And at twelve o'clock the next day, when he opened the door to her, he pulled her into his arms and kissed her. Lunch was completely forgotten by both of them. She wasn't sure who started undressing whom, but there was a trail of clothing from his front door, up the open-tread wooden stairs and through into his bedroom.

The room was almost bare apart from a huge *bateau lit* with pure white linen sheets; there was an uplighter in the corner of the room, what she recognised as a small and extremely expensive stereo system, and a bedside table in the same polished cherry wood as the *bateau lit*. White voile at the huge window let light filter softly into the room.

It was a room built for seduction.

How many women had Alex seduced here?

He stroked her face, as if sensing her tension. 'Tina. If you've changed your mind, that's fine.'

She stared at him, her mouth dry. 'I…don't want to be just another notch.'

'There aren't any notches on my bedpost,' he said

softly. 'You're the only woman who's ever seen the inside of this room. The only woman I've ever asked to share this bed with me.'

Her puzzlement must have shown on her face, because he smiled ruefully. 'It's a long story, and not one I want to tell right now. I won't hold it against you if you back out now. Though my sanity might.'

That last little quirk of humour was enough to dissolve her doubts—at least temporarily—and she stood on tiptoe, reaching up to kiss him. She could feel a shudder ripple through him, and then he lifted her up and carried her to his bed.

CHAPTER NINE

'I'VE fantasised about this since the moment I met you,' Alex said, propping himself up on one elbow and looking down on her. 'You, in my bed, smiling up at me.' He kissed the tip of Tina's nose. 'I wanted to do this.' He kissed the sensitive spot at the curve of her neck. 'And this.' He licked the hollows of her collarbones. 'And this.'

Tina shivered and arched beneath him. 'Alex, I…'

'Me, too,' he said huskily, knowing exactly what she meant even though she hadn't actually said it. He felt more in tune with her than he'd ever felt with anyone before, even Vivi.

He shifted to kiss her properly. Being skin to skin with her was the most incredible feeling in the world. Nothing else existed: just Tina. Every sight was Tina; every scent was Tina; every taste was Tina; every touch was Tina. He never wanted this moment to end. Unless it could co-exist with a thousand other moments that were equally filled with the woman he loved.

He loved her.

The shock hit him like a tidal wave. He loved her. He wanted her with him for the rest of their lives. He wanted her smile to be the first thing he saw when he woke up, the last thing he felt against his skin when he went to sleep. He wanted to hold her and protect her. He wanted to walk along the beach in the middle of winter with her holding her hand and laughing as the wind streamed through their hair. He wanted to splash with their children in a paddling pool on a hot summer's day, build snowmen

114

with them in the middle of winter, listen to her read them stories. And then, when the children were in bed and it was officially their time, he wanted her in his arms.

I love you. Marry me. Have my babies and grow old with me.

He almost said it—but something held him back. He knew she wasn't ready to hear it yet. There was still a long, long way to go before he could call her completely his, before he could ask her—and Josh—to share his life. Until then, maybe he could show her how he felt. Maybe his mouth and hands could give her the message that his mouth dared not.

Making love with Alex was a revelation, Tina thought. It was as if they'd been born to love each other. Although she felt shy, out of practice and nervous in case she did something wrong, Alex drove all her fears and insecurities away by the way he touched her, kissed her, paid attention to every tiny part of her body from the top of her head to the sensitive spot on her instep.

'Touch me,' he whispered hoarsely, and finally she allowed herself to investigate the texture of his skin. The dark hairs on his chest tickled her fingers. She leaned forward and heard his gasp of pleasure as she licked his hard, flat nipples. It gave her the confidence to explore further, sliding her hand down over his hips and cupping his buttocks.

'Have I told you, Dr Bowen, your backside is ravishing?'

No. She hadn't said that, surely? Her face flamed.

Alex just grinned. Broadly. 'Why, thank you, ma'am,' he drawled. He licked her earlobe. 'And your own posterior isn't bad at all, Dr Lawson. Next time I see you in surgery in one of those prissy little suits—' his voice grew even huskier '—I'm going to remind myself of what it's hiding.'

She fell for the bait immediately. 'And what's that?'

'I've already told you. Your delectable body.' He raised her hand to his mouth and drew her little finger between his lips, sucking hard. 'You blow my mind, Tina,' he breathed.

And then he proceeded to blow *her* mind by releasing her hand, dipping his head and performing the same action on her nipple. She arched against the linen sheets, sliding her hands into his hair and urging him on. When she was whimpering with need, he switched his attention to her other breast, paying close attention to her nipple. And when his mouth headed southwards, trailing over her ribcage and navigating her navel in a teasing circle, Tina couldn't stop her hips lifting. She wanted him. Now.

'Alex. *Please*,' she whispered.

By the time he paused to protect her, she was so aroused she felt as if her bones had melted. And when he finally entered her, it was like coming home. She matched him move for move, urging him on. And when she climaxed, it was his face she saw, his name she called out— and her name she heard in his answering cry.

He kissed her gently and withdrew, shifting them both into a more comfortable position. Tina lay on her side, curled against him, her head resting on his shoulder and his arm tightly round her. Her own arm was resting lightly across his body, her hand possessively on his hip.

Possessive. Now, there was a thought. This beautiful, sexy man was all hers. She couldn't remember the last time she'd felt this peaceful, this happy.

And then she heard a sound. Very faint at first, but growing louder. A tinny, musical sound. A tune on a mobile phone: *Humpty Dumpty sat on a wall…*

Her mobile.

She wasn't on duty, so it couldn't be work.

Which meant that something was very, very wrong.

'Alex… I have to answer that,' she said urgently.

He didn't try to stop her, talk her back to bed. He simply climbed out, took a robe from the back of his bedroom door and handed it to her without question. Tina wrapped it round herself and pelted downstairs to answer her phone.

'Hello?'

'Tina?'

The line was bad but Tina could hear the panic in the other woman's voice. 'Susie? What is it?' But even before Susie spoke again, Tina went cold, fear freezing its way up the back of her neck. There was only one thing it could be.

Susie's words confirmed it.

'It's Josh. He's had an accident. We're at—at the hospital now. I'm so sorry—he…' Her words dissolved in crackles.

Tina gripped the phone so tightly her knuckles went white, but she was still shaking. Josh? An accident? How badly was he hurt? Please, God, he wasn't…dead? Not her little boy.

She had just enough presence of mind to say, 'Tell me when I see you. Are you at A and E?'

'Yes. I'm so…' The rest of the word was obscured by line noise, but Tina could guess what it was. An apology. In Susie's shoes, she'd have done the same.

But Josh…

'OK, I'm on my way now.'

Tina turned off her phone and spun round to see Alex there, a towel wrapped loosely around his waist.

'What's happened?'

'Susie's taken Josh to A and E.'

'Is he badly hurt?'

'I don't know. The line was bad.' She swallowed. 'I have to go.'

'I'll drive you.'

She shook her head. 'I'll manage.'

'Tina, don't argue. He's your son and you're worried sick. It's safer if I drive you.'

'I—'

'Get dressed and I'll drive you,' Alex said, his tone brooking no argument.

Tina followed him back upstairs and changed in the bathroom while he dressed in the bedroom. All the while, she kept thinking how this was all her fault. If only she hadn't been so selfish; if only she hadn't asked Susie to take over a responsibility that should have been her own; if only she hadn't given in to her desire and made love with Alex... Then she wouldn't have had the payback of Josh being in hospital. Josh being seriously ill.

Perhaps it was something minor. Perhaps he'd dislocated his elbow or something—he'd done that before, rushing round in a shop and slipping over and banging his arm on a display of cans. But her heart knew that it was a lot more serious than that. Susie had been a childminder for years and she had a son of her own—she knew when not to worry and when to panic. And she had definitely been panicking when she'd spoken to Tina.

Please, God. He's all I've got. He's all I've got left of Rod, Tina thought despairingly. Don't let him die on me, too. Please.

Alex said very little on the drive to Melbury General. The world had just come crashing back into his dream—and not in the best way either. Tina looked pale and stricken, her fingers locked so tightly together that the knuckles stood out white, but he guessed it was more than just worry about her little boy.

No doubt she was blaming herself for being selfish, for making love with him. Somehow, he had to make her see that none of this was her fault. But now wasn't the time. Once she'd found out how badly Josh was hurt, maybe he'd be able to talk to her about it.

Don't let me lose her, he thought, aware that he was being selfish and he ought to be thinking about her little boy instead, but unable to help himself. Now Alex knew what it was like to lie in her arms, to lose himself in her body, he couldn't bear the idea of it never happening again. He wanted her. All of her. Including Josh.

'I'll drop you off here,' he said as he stopped the car in front of the hospital entrance. 'I'll find a parking space and meet you in A and E.'

'No need. I'll manage,' she said brusquely, then, remembering her manners, added, 'Thanks for the lift.'

Alex's face tightened but he merely nodded and drove away.

Tina, adrenalin pumping faster and faster round her body, ran to A and E. 'My friend brought my little boy in,' she told the receptionist. 'Josh Turnbull. Can I see him, please?'

'I'll just get the nurse, Mrs Turnbull.'

Tina didn't bother to correct either her title or her surname. It wasn't important. Nothing was important now, as long as Josh was all right. Please, please, please, God—let him be all right, she prayed silently. I'll never put another foot out of line, never put myself first again. Only let him be all right.

'Mrs Turnbull? This way,' a nurse said.

Tina followed her in silence, her throat too dry and tight

to let her ask the questions she was burning to have answered. Josh was lying on a bed in one of the cubicles, his eyes closed, and Susie was sitting next to him, holding his hand. He had a plaster on one temple and his face was chalk-white with dark circles under his eyes. Susie didn't look much better.

'Susie?' Tina said. She barely recognised her own voice.

'Oh, Tina. I'm so sorry.'

'What happened? Where's Mike?'

'Mike's with my mum. I called her while I was waiting for the ambulance and she's picking him up from school.' Susie swallowed. 'I feel so terrible! It was such a nice day, I thought Josh'd like to go to the park and get some fresh air. He'd been climbing sensibly on the frames, and then he went on the slide. He was at the top and I thought he was going to sit down, except he…' She closed her eyes for a moment, as if reliving the horror. 'He jumped instead of sliding down. He banged his head. He didn't black out but I wasn't going to take a risk with a head injury, not when he'd fallen from that height. I rang the ambulance and then my mum, and they brought him straight here. I tried your mobile but there wasn't any answer.'

No. Because she'd been too busy having sex with Alex.

'I tried you again while they were in X-Ray.'

'Mummy?' Josh opened his eyes.

'I'm here, darling.'

Susie moved away from the bed, leaving room for Tina to sit next to her son.

'I fell off the slide. I'm sorry, Mummy. I didn't mean to.' A tear slid down his face. 'My head hurts.'

'That's because you banged it. But you're in the best place to check you're all right.' The last time she'd been in hospital… No. She wasn't going to think about Rod now. This wasn't the same thing at all. Rod had been dead on arrival at the hospital. Josh was alive and he wasn't going to die. He *couldn't*.

Tina turned to the nurse. 'What tests have you done on him? Is there any cervical spine injury?' Stupid question. Susie had said he'd been to X-Ray and he wasn't still on a spinal board, so obviously she had nothing to worry about there. 'What about his ICP?' Rising ICP or intra-cranial pressure, the most common symptom of which was unequal pupils, could mean a bleed within the brain—and if it wasn't treated urgently the patient could die.

The nurse looked at her in surprise. 'You're a doctor?'

'GP,' Tina confirmed. Though it was a truism that you asked all the questions when your own child was the pa-tient—it was as if you'd forgotten all your training.

'There's no sign of spinal injury, Dr Turnbull, and all the neurological tests have been fine so far, though we'd like to keep him in overnight for observation—we're go-ing to admit him to Paediatrics.'

Tina nodded. Children were much harder to assess than adults, so she knew it was quite routine—although at the same time she was still panicking inside. 'Can I stay with him?'

'Of course. There's a room where parents can get some sleep—or if there's a side room free with a chair-bed in it, you could use that. I'll go and sort out the paperwork.' The nurse smiled and left the cubicle.

'You're going to be all right, darling,' she told Josh, kissing his cheek and stroking his sandy hair off his face. 'I'm here and you'll be fine. Just, next time, come down the slide like everyone else, hmm?' She hoped that the little boy couldn't hear her voice shaking.

'I will, Mummy. I'm tired.'

Drowsiness was common after head injuries. But it was important he stay awake for another hour or so. If he went to sleep, he could lose consciousness. 'I know, darling, but just try to stay awake.' She tightened her fingers round his and looked at Susie. 'Thanks for getting him here.'

'It's my fault he was here in the first place. Look, I understand if you don't ever want me to look after—'

'It's not your fault.' Tina cut her off gently. If it was anyone's fault, it was her own: payback for being selfish, for betraying Rod's memory. 'I should have warned you about Josh and slides.'

'He's done it before?' Susie's face mirrored a mixture of shock and relief.

'He hasn't fallen—but he hasn't been far off,' Tina said. 'Look, your mum'll be worrying and so will Mike. I'll ask the receptionist to sort out a taxi for you—and I'll pay for it.'

'You don't have to do that.'

'It's the least I can do,' Tina insisted.

The curtain round the cubicle swished back and Alex stood there, his face white. 'Tina? How is he?'

'Head injury. They're keeping him in overnight in Paeds to be on the safe side,' Tina said. 'I'm staying with him.' And if she hadn't been with Alex in the first place, Josh wouldn't be here now. It was a sign, she decided. Josh would be fine but she'd have to stay away from Alex. Starting now. 'Thanks for the lift, but you don't need to worry about staying.' A thought struck her. 'In fact… maybe you can give Susie a lift home.'

'I'll get a taxi,' Susie said hastily.

There was a long silence while Alex looked into Tina's eyes, and then he nodded. 'I'm going back to Ellingthorpe anyway, so I'll give you a lift back. Tina, is there anything you want me to bring to the hospital for you?'

'Thanks, but I'll be fine.' Tina forced a smile to her face. 'It's nice to have such a concerned boss.' She emphasised the last word just enough not to alert Susie or Josh, but enough to telegraph the situation to Alex. He was her boss, and that was all he ever could or would be, from now on.

'I'll ring later to see how he is.' He looked tortured, as if he wanted to say something else—but then remembered that Susie was there, and subsided. 'Sure there's nothing you need?'

Tina heard the subtext. And much as she would have loved to have said yes, she needed him, she needed him to hold her and tell her everything was all right, she knew she had to do this on her own. 'Nothing,' she said, telegraphing her own subtext right back. Because 'nothing' had to include Alex himself.

She stayed with Josh while he was admitted to Paediatrics. When she rang her parents to tell them the news, they offered to come over straight away, but she persuaded them not to, promising to call them if there was any change and when she needed a lift home. And then she spent an uncomfortable night on the chair next to Josh's bed, too frightened to doze off in case he slipped into unconsciousness.

The nursing staff did neurological observations every fifteen minutes, checking Josh's pulse, temperature, blood pressure and breathing, as well as his pupils.

'It's all my fault, baby,' she whispered to her sleeping child late in the middle of the night. 'It's my punishment—I should have been concentrating on you instead of betraying your daddy's memory.' And she'd learned her lesson. From now on, she and Alex were going to be colleagues, nothing more.

She was carefully polite and a little cool with him the

next morning when he phoned to see how Josh was. And then it was time for ward rounds.

'And how are you this morning, young man?' the paediatric consultant asked, a twinkle in his grey eyes.

'All right,' Josh said. 'My head doesn't hurt any more.'

'That's good.' The consultant sat on the end of his bed. 'But you scared the life out of your mum, I think.'

'I won't do it *ever* again,' Josh promised.

The consultant's lips twitched. 'Until the next time, hmm?'

'Sounds like you have one like it at home,' Tina said wryly.

'Matthew. Tell me about it.' The consultant rolled his eyes. 'Fourteen months old and a complete terror. He climbs everywhere, terrifies me and his mother—and I think it's worse if you're a doctor,' he said, 'because you automatically think of the worst-case scenario. Did you get any sleep at all last night, Dr Lawson?'

'Not much,' she admitted.

'Well, I've had a word with Sister, and I'm happy with the observations. I think he's been lucky, but you'll need to keep an close eye on him over the next couple of days.'

'And if there's any sign of drowsiness, headache or vomiting, bring him straight back?'

He nodded. 'I'd normally direct parents to their GP if they're worried, but in your case I think you already know what to look for and when to bring him in. So I'll discharge him now.'

'Thanks. I'll ring my parents—they'll pick me up,' Tina said.

They did—and they stayed a bit longer so Tina could grab a couple hours' sleep, after they'd convinced her that they'd wake her if they were even the slightest bit worried about Josh.

Alex called several times, but she let him talk to her answering-machine. To her relief, he was sensitive enough to keep away. She couldn't have handled actually seeing him. Not until she was absolutely sure Josh was going to be all right.

By the middle of the next day, she was beginning to think that she'd been panicking over nothing—and then Josh went quiet on her.

Josh was never quiet and still—not unless he was asleep or ill. Her heart speeded up. 'Joshie? Are you all right?'

'I want to go to bed,' he whispered. 'Sleep.'

No. Please, God, don't let it be what I think it is. Please, just let him be tired. Please. 'Does your head still hurt?' she asked gently, praying that the answer would be no.

'Yes.'

Her heartbeat moved from canter to gallop. 'The same as yesterday, or not as bad?'

'Worse.'

And then he was sick. Violently so.

All the signs pointed to an extradural haemorrhage—bleeding into the space between the skull and the brain, caused by a rupture in an artery next to a fracture in the skull. The blood clotted and caused pressure in the skull, which in turn caused headaches, drowsiness, vomiting, seizures and even partial paralysis; it could take several hours or even days after the original injury for the blood clot to grow and symptoms to show up.

She forced herself to calm down. Maybe she was panicking over nothing. It was like seeing a notice pinned up at school to check your children's head for nits and your scalp itching immediately—you always started assuming the worst. Josh hadn't had a seizure and there were no signs of paralysis.

But she still wasn't taking any chances.

'Joshie, we're going to go back to see the nice doctor at the hospital. We're going now,' she said.

'I wan' go sleep.' His voice sounded slightly slurred.

All Tina's instincts screamed to her to get him into the car and drive—but she couldn't risk it. If he had a seizure while she was driving, there would be nothing she could do. Instead, she rang 999, talked the operator through what the problem was and sat tight.

Within ten minutes—ten minutes which seemed to stretch into ten years—an ambulance was outside her front door and they were loading Josh into the back. She grabbed her handbag and keys, flicked the latch, slammed the door behind her and joined him in the ambulance.

When they got to the hospital, Josh went straight for a CT scan, and the consultant came over to talk to her. 'Dr Lawson, I'm afraid your son has an extradural haemorrhage.' He pointed out the lens-shaped clot on the screen that showed the scan results. 'We need to drill some burr holes in his skull to release the clot, then we'll get him into neurosurgery so they can tie off the bleeding vessel.'

'Can I…can I come in with him?'

He shook his head. 'I'm sorry, Dr Lawson. It's not a good idea. Is there anyone who can sit with you?'

'That doesn't matter right now. Is he going to be all right?'

'You caught it early. He hasn't lost consciousness, he hasn't had a fit, there aren't any signs of hemiparesis—' referring to paralysis on one side of the body '—his breathing's still fine and his pupils don't look too bad. So we're talking best-case scenario,' he said reassuringly.

Even so, Josh could still die. She knew that. If he arrested in Theatre…

He couldn't. *He was all she had.*

'Please…'

He squeezed her hand. 'We'll do our best by him. Has he had anything to eat or drink in the last few hours?'

'A piece of toast and some milk for breakfast. I was about to give him his lunch when he went quiet on me—and then he was sick.'

'So his stomach's probably empty. That's good.'

Tina stayed with Josh while they gave him a pre-med and shaved his hair off. Then she walked down the corridor with him to Theatre, holding his hand—and the Theatre Sister had to ask her four times to let his hand go so they could take him in for his operation.

Unpeeling her hand from his felt like someone had ripped her arm off. She wanted to run to her baby, cradle him in her arms and protect him from the world…but without the operation he'd die.

'I love you, Josh,' she told her unconscious child, and watched the doors swing closed behind the trolley before she sank down on one of the plastic chairs in the corridor. She didn't want to leave her spot to ring her parents in case she missed news about Josh, and she knew better than to use her mobile in a hospital. She wasn't even wearing a watch so she had no idea what the time was.

The waiting seemed to go on for ever, second after dragging second. All the time, Tina kept telling herself that Josh was going to be all right, he was in the best hands. And all the time, she couldn't help thinking, what if?

CHAPTER TEN

ALEX banged on the door. Tina's car was parked outside, so she couldn't have gone far. Maybe she'd taken Josh to feed the ducks. Maybe she'd gone to visit her parents.

But she'd also ignored every single phone message he'd left. And he'd reached the end of his patience. He had to know how Josh was. How *she* was.

He banged on the door again.

'Looking for Tina, are you?' a voice came from the open door of the cottage next to Tina's.

'Yes. Do you know where she's gone?' Alex asked.

The old lady shook her head. 'But there was an ambulance outside, not half an hour ago.'

Josh. 'Thank you,' Alex said, and got straight into his car. A quick phone call—once he'd pulled rank and told the receptionist at A and E he was the family GP, just checking up on the boy—established that Josh Turnbull had been taken to A and E twenty minutes earlier. Josh was having a scan but they couldn't tell him any more than that.

Alex knew exactly what they were looking for. And if they found it...Tina would need someone with her. He switched off his mobile phone and drove straight to the hospital.

Please, let him live. Please, let him live.

'Tina.'

She looked up at Alex and her eyes dilated with shock. 'What are you doing here?'

'You didn't answer the phone. I was worried—and when I called by, your neighbour told me there'd been an ambulance outside. I guessed you'd be here. What's happened?'

'Josh had an extradural bleed.' She had no idea how she managed to get the words out—how she managed to sound so calm. Inside, she was a screaming, sobbing wreck. 'They're doing a craniotomy now so I should hear something soon.'

'Are you all right?'

No. What she really wanted to do was to fling herself into his arms and sob her heart out on his shoulder, but she couldn't. If she hadn't been thinking of herself in the first place, Josh wouldn't be here now. 'I'm fine,' she lied.

'Can I get you anything? A coffee? A sandwich?'

She shook her head. 'Nothing, thanks. I couldn't eat anyway.' Her throat felt as if she'd swallowed a ton of sawdust, swollen from the tears she'd forced back.

'Tina...'

'I'm OK on my own,' she said carefully.

He moved as if to put his arm round her and she put up one hand to ward him off. 'No, Alex. We can't.'

Alex stared at her. In her shoes, he'd have wanted someone with him. Someone to grieve with, someone to be strong and hold him and reassure him everything was going to be all right. He knew she was strong—but not *that* strong. Why was she pushing him away now?

Unless...she was blaming him for what had happened to Josh. Or, worse still, blaming herself. 'Tina, it's not either of our faults he's here,' he said gently.

'Isn't it?' Her mouth twisted bitterly. 'If I'd been doing what any other decent mother had done—looking after my son myself, instead of dumping him on a childminder while I swanned off to enjoy myself—he'd be fine now.'

'Or you'd have been there as he fell and blamed yourself for not catching him,' Alex countered.

'No. I put myself first, and this is what I get for being selfish. I'm going to lose him, too. Now, please—just go.'

Being selfish? Losing Josh too? The fears he'd had when he'd driven her to A and E to see Josh became frighteningly real. Tina was feeling guilty, regretting what they'd done together. Partly because of Rod. And he was going to lose her.

Don't give up now, whispered the imp. *You know it's not her fault; she needs to know it too. Tell her.* He took a deep breath. 'Tina, I didn't know Rod, but if he loved you half as much as you loved him, he'd have wanted you to be happy. So this isn't a punishment for what happened between you and me, or just deserts, or anything like that—it was an accident, and it could have happened at any time.'

'This isn't the time or the place to argue,' she said, her voice clipped.

'Agreed.'

'So just leave me—please?'

He didn't want to leave her. His whole body was screaming out to hold her close, to give her his strength, and the imp was urging him on. But if he pushed her too hard now, she'd break. He had to back off…for now. 'If that's what you really want. Do your parents know you're here?'

She shook her head. 'I…'

He guessed what she meant. She wanted to ring but she didn't dare leave her post in case she missed talking to the surgeon, yet if she didn't ring her parents would be hurt that she hadn't told them. Whatever she did would be wrong and she'd be torn with guilt. 'I'll ring them for you, if you like—or call in on them on the way home.'

He could see the conflict in her face—she felt she ought to be the one to break the bad news, and letting him do it would be too much like letting him take over some of her responsibility. And yet not telling her parents was equally unfair.

'I'll tell them,' he said softly. 'Call me if you need me.'

And if she didn't call him at all? He'd deal with that when the time came. He squeezed her shoulder comfortingly, and left.

The next few hours were the longest of Tina's life. She paced up and down the corridor outside Theatre, clenching and unclenching her fists as she walked. Josh had to be all right. He *had* to be.

And then at last the neurosurgeon came out to see her.

She couldn't tell immediately from his face: was it good news or bad? Had the operation been a success, or had he found something terrible once he'd drilled the burr holes and lifted the lid of bone away to repair the ruptured blood vessel in Josh's brain?

'Dr Lawson?'

'Yes. How's Josh?'

He smiled at her. 'I'm pleased to tell you that the operation was a success. I've removed the clot, located the bleed and clipped the blood vessel—and because you caught him right at the early stages, he's going to be fine.'

'Oh, thank God,' she said.

He squeezed her hand. 'We'll keep him in for a week, but he'll be in a side room and you're welcome to stay with him as much as you'd like. He'll have a few headaches for a while, but nothing too serious. He's going to be fine.'

'Thank you,' she said—and promptly burst into tears of relief.

*   *   *

Alex sent a message via Tina's parents to let her know that he'd arranged a locum to cover for her—a locum to cover a locum, she thought wryly—and there was no pressure, but the surgery would be happy to have her back whenever she felt able to join them again. He also sent gifts for Josh via her parents—puzzles, a book on rockets with some pictures that Josh declared were 'awesome', a piece of Icelandic spar that made everything appear double, and a piece of sand-coloured shale containing a tiny black fish fossil called a *knightia*. But no more messages for her—he'd done what she'd asked and backed off.

Tina spent her days and nights at the hospital, not wanting to leave her son for a single minute. Her parents persuaded her to take the odd hour's rest while they sat with Josh, but otherwise she didn't leave her little boy's side.

On Josh's fourth day in hospital, while he was asleep, she had a surprise visitor, bearing a box of Belgian chocolate seashells.

'I remembered what you told me and thought these might help,' Jan said softly.

Tina gave her a watery smile. 'Thanks. And thanks for coming, especially after…' Her voice faded. It was hardly tactful to remind Jan of her own problems.

'I nearly turned back at the doors,' Jan admitted. 'Though at least the ward isn't in the same block as Maternity. I don't think I could have come if it had been.' She looked at the sleeping child. 'How is he?'

'On the mend.' Tina rubbed her hand across her eyes. 'Though I think I've aged about a hundred years in the last few days.'

'Hey.' Jan gave her a hug. 'You'll do.'

'So how are things with you?' Tina asked as her friend sat down in the other armchair.

'I've got to come to terms with the fact I'll never have a child of my own. I'll never have the worry you've just had—but I'll never have the joy either.' Jan sighed. 'Though Dr Bowen's been marvellous.'

Alex. Tina forced back the swell of longing that rippled through her at the sound of his name. Alex was forbidden fruit.

'He's dropped in to see me most days, just for a quick chat and to see how I am. And he's made me realise that the longer I spend hiding at home, the worse it's going to be when I finally go back to work and face everyone. I was thinking about changing my career, but he's right. I'm good at what I do and I enjoy it—going into an office instead would be like cutting off my nose to spite my face and I'd be miserable.' Jan shrugged. 'I might look into doing some more training, though—become a fully qualified teacher rather than staying as a classroom assistant.'

'Good for you,' Tina said. 'And if you feel like doing some private tuition over the next few weeks, once Josh is up to doing schoolwork again, let me know. Or if you'd rather not, if you can recommend someone who can help me keep him up with the rest of his class, I'd really appreciate it.'

'No, I'd love to do it. Poor little mite.' Jan looked at Josh and smiled. 'Oh, the little darling. That baby fuzz growing back…'

'He cried when he realised all his hair had been shaved off for the operation—until I told him that all superheroes had their hair cut off at some point. Though on the other hand I might have put more ideas into his head,' Tina said ruefully. 'One thing's for sure, he's never going on another slide again.' She stroked Josh's hand. 'Ever.'

Finally, Josh was allowed home. Tina's father drove them extremely slowly back to Ellingthorpe, and Tina agonised over every tiny little bump.

Tina's mum was waiting for them, and the cottage smelled gorgeous—fresh-baked bread and home-made burgers to tempt Josh. 'Thanks, Mum.'

'I've done some batch-baking and filled your freezer, too—all you have to do is take the dish out the night before, thaw it and reheat it.'

Tina hugged her mother, knowing Shirley had guessed that she wouldn't want to spend a single moment away from Josh unless she really, really had to and would begrudge every second she had to spend in the kitchen. 'Thanks.' She swallowed back her tears. 'I really appreciate it.' The whole place was tidy—sparkling, even. She couldn't remember the last time it had looked this good. 'Though you didn't have to do all my housework as well.'

'Tina, you've got enough on your plate without having to worry about cooking. And I'm not the one you need to thank for the housework anyway,' Shirley said.

Tina frowned. 'Who, then?'

'We'll talk about it later,' Shirley said evasively. 'Right now, the important thing's to get Josh settled in again.'

The little boy ate sparsely, but it was more than he'd eaten while in hospital. The ice cream tempted him a little more—together with some strawberries from his grandfather's greenhouse—and then he curled up in Tina's arms and went to sleep.

When Tina had carried him to bed and pulled the duvet over him, Shirley dropped the bombshell. 'Alex Bowen did the housework for you.'

'*Alex?*' Tina echoed in a horrified whisper. 'But—how?'

'The usual way, I expect.'

Tina gave her mother an evil glare, which simply made

Shirley grin. 'He wanted to do something practical to help. I said he could water your plants—and he decided to go one step further.'

'He's my boss,' Tina muttered.

Though the look in her mother's eyes made her think that maybe Shirley saw Alex as more than just a concerned colleague—or even a friend.

'He's a nice man, love.'

'The rest of my colleagues at the surgery are nice, too,' Tina shot back.

Shirley said nothing, but Tina knew her mother had guessed what had happened between them—was sympathetic even. But Tina wasn't ready to hear that life had to go on, Rod would have wanted her to be happy and the like. She'd already had that from Alex himself. And she still couldn't help thinking that if she hadn't been so selfish and given in to her body's demands, Josh wouldn't be lying here now, a bandage round his shaven head.

About an hour after her parents had left, while she was leafing through a magazine at Josh's bedside with most of her attention on the little boy, her doorbell rang.

Alex.

They were going to be friends, and friends only, she reminded herself. And it probably wasn't him anyway. It was probably Rose next door, seeing if she wanted anything. Or someone from the surgery. Josh's teacher. Any of a dozen, twenty people.

But when she opened the door and saw Alex, the rush of desire was so strong she almost had to sit down on the spot. She managed to pull herself together—just—but she didn't trust herself to speak.

'Hello, Tina. Can I…um…come in?'

For a moment she almost said no. Having him so close

to her and knowing that she couldn't be with him, would never share those moments of passion with him again, would be torture. But then politeness prevailed and she stood aside to let him in.

'Would you like a coffee?' she asked.

'No, thanks. It's just a flying visit to see how Josh is.'

'He's asleep upstairs at the moment, but he's on the mend.' She paused and her throat dried. 'Thanks for what you did here.'

'No problem.' He paused. 'How are you?'

'I'm fine.'

Their eyes had a rather different conversation.

I'm not fine. I need a hug.

Ask me and it's yours. I'll hold you for ever.

I can't.

I'm not going to push you. If you want my arms round you, then tell me. I'm here. But only if you ask me.

I can't.

There was a long, long silence. Actually, it was probably only seconds, but it felt like hours to Tina. 'Jan came to see me at the hospital,' she said. 'She's going back to work.'

'That's the best thing she could do. I've talked to her about other possibilities—adoption, or even long-term fostering. She said she'll think about it.'

'Good. Has Walter Pearmain been in?'

'No, but the health visitor's kept me informed and I've had the first set of liver-function test results back. We've traced all his contacts and arranged their heaf tests, and Walter's doing well.'

The imp was frantically hopping up and down on his shoulder and finally regained control of his mouth. 'When are you coming back?'

She folded her arms. 'For heaven's sake! I've only just brought Josh home. He's on bed rest right now.'

'Which will drive him crazy—and you even more so if you don't get a break.'

Her eyes narrowed. 'So what are you suggesting?'

Make or break time, Alex thought. When Bethany had died, he'd made the mistake of letting distance build between himself and Vivi. He wasn't going to make that mistake again. He wanted Tina and he knew she wanted him. Right now, he guessed that she felt guilty and confused and miserable, she'd barely slept for a week and was worried sick about Josh—but he wasn't going to back off completely and let her build those feelings into an insurmountable wall between them.

He took a deep breath. 'You know we're looking for a new partner at the surgery. We discussed it this morning and none of the applicants were suitable, so we're changing our requirements. We're looking for a part-time partner.'

She stared blankly at him.

'*You*, Tina,' he said. 'We want you to join us as a part-time partner.'

'Me?'

'You,' he confirmed. 'You're a good doctor, you fit in well with the rest of us and the patients adore you.'

'But—'

'I know you need to spend more time with Josh right now. We've got a locum to cover for you. But we want you back, permanently, when you're ready.' He tipped his head slightly to one side. 'I thought you could come back maybe one morning a week to start with, and work up to more sessions as Josh gets better.'

Her face set. 'I can't leave Josh.'

'How about if you had a qualified doctor watching him?'

She frowned. 'What?'

'Me,' he explained. 'I'll stay with him while you're at the surgery.'

'But…won't you be at the surgery, too?'

'I'll change my hours to fit round yours.'

'But…' She shook her head slowly, as if not quite believing what she was hearing.

'Tina, don't be stubborn about this. You need all the support you can get—Josh has been through a lot, and so have you. But you don't have to do it all on your own.' He took a deep breath. 'So, until Josh is better, I'm suggesting you have a house guest.'

'What?' She frowned, looking completely confused.

'Me,' he said. 'I'm going to take turns in sitting with Josh so you get a break—and that's nights as well as days, so I'm commandeering your sofa.'

Her face set. 'He's *my* son.'

'And he's my friend—*you're* my friend,' Alex countered. 'Friends do things for each other.'

Her eyes narrowed. 'We can't—'

'This isn't about you and me.' Well, it was and it wasn't. 'And it's not a way of trying to seduce you either.' Yes, he wanted to make love with her again and again, for the rest of his life—but only as a willing partner. He wasn't going to push her into something she wasn't ready for yet. But he was going to make damned sure he was there when she *was*. 'It's about a little boy whose mother's about to run herself into the ground. And if you do that, you're not going to be in a fit state to look after him. So you have to accept help—for Josh's sake.'

'And you'd do this for all your friends?' she tested.

'What do you think?' he asked softly.

If she said yes, she'd have to accept his help and she'd grow used to him being in her life—maybe enough to let him stay there permanently. If she said no, she'd be forced to admit to the attraction between them. Either way, they both won.

She sighed. 'OK—I mean, thanks for the offer. You're right. I can't do it all on my own. But you can't sleep on my sofa—you're too tall and it'll do your back in. I'll sleep with Josh and you can have my room.'

'We're taking turns with Josh, and that includes nights,' he reminded her.

Alex wished she hadn't said that about having her room. The idea of sleeping in her bed was playing havoc with his heartbeat. Especially since she would be just the other side of the wall. It didn't take a huge stretch for his imagination to dream her there with him.

She raked a hand through her hair. 'We'll work something out.'

Good. She was beginning to compromise at last. Maybe there was hope for them. But one thing was for sure, he wasn't going to give up on her, the way he had with Vivi.

'I'll go and get my stuff, then, shall I?' he said.

Tina was silent for a long, long time. And then she nodded.

CHAPTER ELEVEN

OVER the next few days, Tina realised that Alex had meant what he'd said: he was offering her friendship and support. His eyes told her a different story—the desire he'd felt for her, the passion they'd shared, was still there—but he kept his hands off her.

Until one evening when she was sitting by Josh's bed, just watching him sleep, and Alex tiptoed into the room.

'What's up?' she asked.

'You,' he said. 'I know you're worried, but you don't have to be with him every second of the day.'

'What if...?' The question stuck in her throat.

He guessed what she hadn't been able to voice. 'It's not going to happen, Tina. He'll be fine now. But if you're with him every second of the day, he's going to start losing confidence and he's going to find it hard to go back to school—maybe even to set foot outside if you're not there, holding his hand.'

She hadn't thought of that. 'Oh.' She bit her lip.

'Come on. Downstairs. Just for half an hour,' he coaxed.

Which was how she found herself sitting next to him on the sofa, a soothing Bach CD on the stereo system and a glass of chilled white wine in her hand. And somehow it ended up with her lying back against him, his arm round her shoulders, her feet on the arm of the sofa and his cheek resting against her hair. No pressure, no demands— and she actually felt safe enough to close her eyes and relax.

It was more like forty minutes later when he pressed a brief kiss against her hair. 'OK. You can go back to Josh now if you want to. But I just wanted to prove to you that he'll be perfectly all right if you take your eyes off him for a few minutes now and again.'

Tina refused to admit that he was right, but the next morning Alex raised the partnership issue again.

'I meant it. We're offering you the job, part time, and your hours can be negotiable to fit around Josh.'

'Thanks.'

'Starting Monday morning.'

Monday? She panicked. It was too soon.

'You need to build your confidence up, too, and learn to let Josh stand on his own two feet again,' he said gently, as if her fears were written in huge letters on her face. 'I'll be with him every second that you're not. And although I'm not going to wrap him in cotton wool, I'll make sure he's OK. I won't let him do anything risky.'

Eventually, she agreed, and she discovered on the following Monday morning that Alex was right. Working, even just for one morning, took her focus off Josh for long enough to relax her, so when she came home again she was less tense and Josh was more relaxed around her as well.

Josh was recovering quickly, and he was enjoying having Alex around the place. Someone to teach him chess, help him make volcanoes out of bicarbonate of soda and vinegar, and build a kite with him. Someone to be a father figure…

No. Stop this right now, Tina told herself. Alex is just a friend.

But what if…?

What *nothing*. Friends. That was the agreement. Just friends.

Even though every evening now she sat with Alex for an hour after Josh had fallen asleep, listening quietly to music and relaxing against him, it was just as friends. The fact she meshed her fingers with his was irrelevant.

Who was she trying to kid?

Late at night, it was driving her insane, knowing that Alex was sleeping in her bed, his body warming her sheets, his skin scenting her pillow. On the nights when he was Josh-sitting and she was sleeping in her own bed, it was even worse—because she could imagine Alex being there beside her.

He felt it, too. She knew he did. She could see it in his face—the dark flare of desire in his eyes, quickly masked, every time he looked at her. And in his mouth, that sensual quirk to his lips. That one afternoon they'd shared, skin to skin, was burned in her memory. She could remember how he'd felt against her, how he'd tasted—everything. And knowing that he was only a few feet away…

It would be so, so easy to give in to it. To walk into the room where he was sleeping, let her robe slip to the floor and offer herself to him. Or even to turn to him when they had that quiet time together in the evening—lift his hand to her mouth and suck each fingertip in turn, the way he'd done to her.

But what would happen afterwards? It would end at some time. It had to. And the effect it would have upon Josh didn't bear thinking about.

So it was easier not to take the risk.

Every day, Josh grew a little better. Tina was just beginning to relax again when the bombshell dropped. In a completely unexpected place.

She'd just brought Josh a cup of warm milk.

'I love you, Mummy,' he said, cuddling against her.

'I love you, too.'

'Mummy...' Here we go, she thought. The days at home were beginning to pall. No doubt he was going to ask if he could go back to school and play with his friends.

'Can Alex be my new daddy?'

She wasn't sure she'd heard right at first. Alex, his new daddy? Then it sank in, and she went rigid. What had Alex been saying to him? 'Alex is just our friend,' she said carefully.

'But he could be my new daddy if you got married to him.'

Her temper began to sizzle. Rod was Josh's father, not Alex! How dared he even suggest taking Rod's place in Josh's life? 'Well, we're not getting married,' she said tightly.

'Why not?'

She'd always sworn she'd explain things properly to her child, not act the way Rod's parents had. But then she heard the dreaded words come out. 'Because I say so.'

He had a mutinous look on his face she recognised, and she raged inwardly. How dared Alex put her in this position? 'Darling, people don't get married just like that. Now, I'll read you a story now and then it's time to sleep.'

'Don't want you to read it. I want Alex.' Josh pouted.

She only just managed to keep her temper in check. 'Alex is busy. He's out on a call.' And when he got back, she'd roast him alive!

'Oh-h-h.' Josh dragged the words out into a whining three syllables, and she kissed the top of his head.

'Come on. Story, then sleep.'

*   *   *

By the time Alex came back from his call-out, after Josh had gone to sleep, Tina's temper erupted.

'What the *hell* have you been saying to him?'

Alex frowned. 'What?'

'Josh. What have you been saying to him?' she demanded.

'I don't know what you're talking about.'

'Yes, you do. You're using him to get to me.'

'Tina—'

'When did you ask him if he'd like you to be his new daddy, then?'

'What?' Alex's jaw dropped. 'I haven't said anything of the sort.'

'Why else would he suggest it?'

'I don't know.' He raked a hand through his hair. 'Tina, can we discuss this later?'

'No, we can *not*. You know what we agreed. Friends. And now Josh wants me to marry you!' She shook her head. 'It's not fair. You're raising his hopes when you know it's not an option. I want my key back, and I want you back in your own house. Now. You've got ten minutes to pack.'

'Tina, don't you think you're over—?' he began.

'No, I am *not* overreacting!' she yelled, stamping her foot.

'Look, you're tired and so am I. Let's talk about this tomorrow when we're both feeling more reasonable.'

'I want you to go, and I want you to go now!' she snarled.

Alex's own temper snapped. 'Fine. Suit yourself!' he snarled back.

Ten minutes later, he was gone.

It was the end, Tina thought two days later. Two miserable days, when Josh had cried and asked for Alex and refused to accept her excuses that Alex was working, that other people needed him.

'But *I* need him, Mummy,' Josh sobbed.

You cow. You complete and utter cow, she said to herself. If you hadn't let Alex get this close in the first place, you wouldn't have this problem now. Your son's breaking his heart over Alex and it should *never* have happened.

She refused to listen to the small, rational voice that pointed out that *she'd* been the one to end it all, not Alex, so the problem had actually been of her making, not his.

Or to the even quieter voice that pointed out she missed him as much as Josh did.

Later that evening, Tina wrote her resignation letter. While her mother sat with Josh, Tina walked down to the surgery and posted it through the letter-box. Tomorrow, she decided, she'd start approaching magazines and big websites, asking them if they needed a medical journalist.

Though she didn't get the chance.

At half past seven the next morning, someone leaned on her doorbell. And continued to lean on it until she opened the door.

'Hello, Alex,' she muttered, not meeting his eyes.

'What is *this* supposed to be?' he demanded, waving her letter under her nose.

'My resignation.'

'I refuse to accept it.'

She lifted her chin to glare at him. 'You can't do that.'

'Yes, I can. I'm the senior partner and I'm pulling rank.'

'Keep your voice down! You'll wake Josh,' she hissed.

He lowered his voice, but his anger was still obvious

in the dark slashes of colour across his cheekbones. 'How is he?'

'Fine.'

Alex gave her a look as if he didn't believe her, but didn't press the point. 'Can we have a rational discussion about this?'

Tina flinched, but knew she deserved the comment. She hadn't exactly been rational the night she'd told him to leave. 'Do you want a coffee?'

He shook his head.

'How come you were at work so early, anyway?' The question was out before she could stop it.

'Why do you think?' he asked softly.

She flushed and refused to answer, standing aside to let him in, then closing the door behind him.

He followed her into the kitchen and leaned back against the worktop, folding his arms. 'I'm not accepting your resignation, Tina. Number one, Josh is happy and settled at school—if you leave the village to work somewhere else, he'll have to start all over again.'

'I could commute.'

His face showed what he thought of that idea. And he was right: how likely was it that she'd find another locum post which could fit round Josh's timetable?

'Number two, we're both adults. We can work together.'

'Yeah, right.'

'I can be professional about it, even if you can't.'

Her temper flared. 'Are you saying I'm not professional?'

'No. Yes. No.' He sighed and raked a hand through his hair. 'I can't think straight any more.'

She wished he hadn't done the thing with his hair. It made him look rumpled. Sexily rumpled. And sexy wasn't a concept she wanted to dwell on right now. Not with Alex close, so close she could smell the clean male scent of his skin. It made her want to press against him, breathe in his scent until she was drunk on it.

'Tina, where did it all go wrong? We were good friends.'

'Were we?'

He held her gaze. 'Until that afternoon, you mean.'

She nodded. 'And that's the problem. I can't work with you,' she said. 'I can't work with you and pretend that afternoon never happened.'

There was a long, long pause. 'Then don't,' he said quietly.

But…hadn't he just said that he wasn't going to accept her resignation? Or had he just changed his mind? 'I don't understand,' she blurted out.

'Don't pretend it never happened.'

'How?'

He held out his arms. 'Easy. Come here.'

'I can't, Alex.'

'What happened between us—whatever you're thinking, I don't collect scalps. I've barely looked at a woman for the past six years; I regarded myself as a doctor first, last and always. Then you walked into my life and blew all my ideas out of the water. I wanted you so badly— purple hair and all. And that afternoon when we made love—it was like being complete again, after years of living only half a life. Like the sun coming out after a month of rainy days.' His eyes were very dark, very serious. 'It's the same for you, isn't it?'

'No,' she lied.

He folded his arms. 'Admit it, Tina. It's not one-sided. I know you're mourning Rod, but there's still something between you and me. Your hands shake whenever I touch you. Your eyes are telling me all sorts of things. And if I ignored your protests and kissed you, you'd be kissing me back.'

Kissing. Oh, lord. Why had he reminded her of how it felt to be in his arms, to feel his mouth against hers? To feel his mouth against other parts of her skin, until she was almost drowning in desire and need for him?

She swallowed. 'All right. I feel it, too.'

'Then let's give it a try. Together.'

Her voice cracked. 'I can't.'

'Why? Rod?'

'It's barely been a year. I...I loved him, Alex.'

'I know you did. You still do. You always will. He was an important part of your life—the father of your child. But there's room for both of us.'

Her tongue felt as if it was stuck to the roof of her mouth and she could hardly talk. 'Is there?'

'*Yes.*' At her doubtful glance, he continued, 'OK, let's try looking at this another way. You loved Rod. Now, put yourself in his shoes. If he'd been the one left behind, would you have wanted him to be on his own for the rest of his life?'

She shook her head.

'Exactly. And if he loved you anywhere near as much as you loved him, he'd understand.'

'It's not just Rod. There's Josh. I can't risk it, Alex— what if it doesn't work out between us? He's already lost his father. I don't want him having a string of ''uncles'' who come into his life and disappear again, letting him down just when he's used to having them around. I can't wreck his life like that.'

Alex smiled at that, reaching out to brush her jawline with his thumb. 'Tina, you're not the sort who flits from man to man. He won't have a string of uncles—just *me*.

I know you come as a package, and that's fine by me. I love him, too. I want us to be a family.'

A family. Her, Alex and Josh. The stuff dreams were made of. But what if…? She shivered. 'I—I need time to think about this, Alex.'

He nodded. 'I'll give you space. But think about it seriously, Tina. Don't just panic and dismiss it as unworkable.'

Don't let her start thinking, you fool! screamed the imp, jumping up and down on his shoulder in a panic. *You know what'll happen if she starts thinking and stops feeling. She'll back off and you'll lose her. It's time you reminded her what she's missing. What you're* both *missing.*

And Alex leaned forward and kissed her. Very gently, very lightly, just brushing his lips across hers. Tina gasped, and he took full advantage, pulling her closer and kissing her properly. Her hands tangled in his hair and somehow his hands were working their way under her T-shirt, his thumbs brushing her nipples through the lace of her bra.

He broke the kiss and looked at her. Her eyes were almost black, rimmed with a tiny hint of violet-blue. Her mouth was reddened and slightly swollen, and her cheeks were flushed. And he'd never, ever seen such a desirable sight.

'I'm going back to the surgery,' he told her hoarsely, 'while I can still be responsible for my actions. But I meant what I said. I want you *and* Josh. I want us to be a real family.' He took her hand and pressed a kiss into her palm, folding her fingers on top. 'I'll see you later this afternoon. Let's talk about it then.'

Not trusting herself to speak, Tina nodded shakily. When she'd closed the front door behind him, she sat down at the kitchen table, her head in her hands. What had he meant by 'I love Josh, too?' You love Josh and so do I? Or I love Josh and I love you?

Because he'd never mentioned love to her.

Not once.

Desire, yes. He'd told her he wanted her—*shown* her how much he wanted her even. But he'd never actually said he loved her.

On the other hand, why else would he have stayed with her, shared the worry of caring for Josh during his recovery?

She sighed. He'd bounced the question back at her when she'd asked if he'd do that kind of thing for all his friends. She still didn't really know the answer. She didn't really *know* Alex. It had all happened so fast. Too fast.

And there were an awful lot of unanswered questions. Maggie had said he'd been married once, but he was divorced when he came to Ellingthorpe. When she'd asked Alex himself, he'd put her off, saying that it was a long story he didn't want to discuss.

Maybe the scars were still raw. And not everyone was as open as she was.

I want you and *Josh*.

She steepled her fingers. If only he'd used the L-word. Or maybe he was scared that she'd fling it back in his face. Hadn't she already thrown him out once, when she'd accused him of using Josh to get to her?

Then again, she hadn't told him she loved him either.

Love. *Did* she love Alex? Stupid question. Of course she did. She loved everything about him—heart, mind, body and soul. She felt guilty about it—surely she should be mourning Rod for longer than twelve months—but she'd never felt a pull like this before.

I want us to be a real family.

Part of her was screaming, *Yes!* And yet it was a risk—a risk to Josh as well as herself. Dared she take it, when she didn't really know how Alex felt about her?

CHAPTER TWELVE

TINA still hadn't come to a decision by mid-morning, when the postman arrived with a parcel for her elderly neighbour, Rose.

'She's usually in around this time, but maybe she didn't hear the doorbell. I knocked a couple of times in case the doorbell batteries had gone or something, but she's not answering the door,' Mel Blake explained. 'Would you mind taking this in for her?'

'Of course not,' Tina said, signing for the parcel. She tried delivering it herself half an hour later, but there was no reply to the doorbell or her knock. She scribbled a note and stuck it through the door to let Rose know that she'd taken in a parcel for her, but when her elderly neighbour still hadn't come round to collect it an hour later, Tina began to worry. Rose always stuck to a routine—this wasn't like her at all.

There was still no answer from the front door, but when Tina tried knocking on the kitchen door at the back of the house, she heard a faint cry. She peered through the kitchen window and saw Rose lying on the floor, still in her nightdress. Maybe the old lady had broken something when she'd fallen and that was why she hadn't been able to get up. Heaven knew how long she'd been lying there. Tina twisted the doorhandle but it refused to budge—locked, she decided. She had to get help, and fast. If Rose had been lying there all night, her body temperature would be dangerously low. There wasn't time to wait for the fire brigade.

She banged on the window. 'Rose! I'll be back in a moment!' She took the parcel back to her own house, told Josh to stay put in front of the film he was watching, grabbed her mobile phone, a thick hand towel and the hammer from her toolkit in the cupboard under the kitchen sink, and went back to Rose's kitchen door.

Thirty seconds later, she'd knocked out the pane of glass just above the doorhandle. The towel protected her hand from injury from the remaining shards of glass, and she was able to reach in and unlock the door from the inside.

'Rose! What happened?' she asked.

'Tripped and fell. I can't get up, Tina.'

At least Rose was talking normally, which meant she wasn't drowsy or confused, two of the possible signs of hypothermia. Her face wasn't pale or puffy either, Tina thought with relief. And when she slipped her hand into the old lady's armpit to check for warmth, the coolness she was dreading wasn't there. With hypothermia, areas of the body that were usually warm, such as the armpits, became cold. If Rose was suffering from it at all, it was still at the mild early stages.

'Where does it hurt?' she asked.

'My side.'

Which probably meant the old lady had fractured her hip. 'I'm not going to move you,' Tina said, 'because I think you might have broken something and I could do a lot more damage if I move you. But I'll try to make you more comfortable.'

'I'm so thirsty,' Rose whispered.

'I can't give you a drink, Rose,' Tina said, 'in case you need to go to Theatre. How long have you been lying there?'

'Half the night. I only wanted a drink of water,' Rose said.

'I'll get help—right now.' Tina dialled the emergency line on her mobile phone, explained the problem to the controller and gave directions for the ambulance to Rose's house. 'They'll be here in a few minutes,' she said. 'Meanwhile, we need to keep you warm.' She went into the living room and took a couple of cushions, then paused in the hallway on her way back to grab a coat and a hat. What she really wanted was a space blanket, heat-reflecting material that would warm the elderly woman gradually—rapid warming made the blood rush to the surface of the body and reduced the blood supply to the heart and brain, which could prove fatal to the elderly. But she didn't have a space blanket in her bag next door. She could ring the practice and ask Lorraine to get one sent over—but the ambulance would probably arrive before anyone could get here from the surgery.

On her way back to Rose's side, she rang her mother on the mobile. 'Mum, can I ask a huge favour? My neighbour's had a fall—I'm with her now and Josh has promised not to move from in front of the telly, but could you come over and watch him for me, please—just until I've settled Rose?'

'Of course I will, love. I'm on my way now.'

'Thanks, Mum.' Tina cut the connection and arranged the coat over the old lady, then gently lifted her head enough to pull the hat on and slipped a cushion underneath her to make the old lady more comfortable.

'A hat? Indoors?' Rose queried.

'You lose nearly a fifth of your body heat from your head,' Tina explained. 'It's just a safeguard. You're stuck here in one position, and I don't want you to end up with hypothermia.'

'I feel silly with a hat on,' Rose muttered.

Tina grinned. 'Not as silly as I did the day I sprayed my hair purple—and then found it wouldn't wash out.'

To her relief, Rose smiled back.

'The ambulance will be here soon,' Tina said, settling down next to Rose and holding her hand. 'Mum's coming to sit with Josh, and I'll ring someone to get your window repaired today. If they can't do it right away, I'll board it up so the house is safe.'

'Thanks, love.' Rose's fingers tightened round hers. 'I don't know what I'd have done if you hadn't found me.'

Even in late spring, the elderly could suffer hypothermia. Half a night lying immobile on a cold kitchen floor had already lowered Rose's temperature. Another day of it… Tina knew exactly what would have happened next. Rose's breathing would have become slow and shallow, she'd have fallen unconscious, her heartbeat would have become slower and more irregular as her body temperature dropped, and it would finally have stopped beating altogether.

But Tina had found her in time. Although she couldn't move the old lady to a sitting position and give her a warm drink, because of the possible fracture, she could at least prevent any further heat loss.

'Funny, lying here, I couldn't stop thinking about Bill.'

'Who's Bill?' Tina asked quietly.

'My fiancé. Well, he wanted to marry me, but all my family were dead set against the match. My friends, too— they all said he wasn't good enough for me. I listened to them and broke off the engagement… I often wonder what would have happened if I'd been braver and taken the risk. Though I'll never know.'

'Did he marry someone else?' Tina asked.

'No. He was killed in the war, the week after I'd given

him his ring back. I often wonder if it was my fault—if he'd have taken more care, had the will to survive, knowing that I was waiting for him.'

'Of course not,' Tina said comfortingly. 'You can't blame yourself.'

'I should have taken the risk,' Rose said. 'I would have had children, then—grandchildren, even—instead of being on my own. My family would have come round to the idea in the end. And if they hadn't, I'd still have had Bill. He would have been enough for me—he'd have been the only family I needed.' She smiled sadly. 'My poor Bill. There never was anyone to match him. If I had my time again, I'd have taken the risk and married him.'

This could be me, in forty years' time, Tina thought. Wishing I'd taken the risk and gone to Alex, given Josh the chance of being part of a real family again. She squeezed Rose's fingers. The old lady was right. Sometimes you had to take the chance.

She'd tell Alex this afternoon. Or even before.

A rap on the door heralded the ambulance crew. 'I'll let them in,' she told Rose. When she opened the door, she could see her mother's car parked in the road outside her house, so Josh was safe. 'Would you like me to come with you in the ambulance?' she offered as the paramedics gently lifted Rose onto the trolley.

'No, love. I've been on my own all these years. I'll be fine on my own now.'

There was a slightly forlorn note beneath the bravery, but Tina knew not to push. Ever since she'd known Rose, the old lady had always been fiercely independent, rarely even letting Tina fetch her something from the shops.

Rose allowed Tina to see her into the ambulance, but no more.

'I'll come to see you later today,' Tina promised. 'Once

your window's repaired. And I'll keep an eye on the cottage for you.'

'The front-door key's in the biscuit barrel,' Rose said. 'I'll keep it safe for you.'

If I had my time again, I'd have taken the risk…

And after that, the decision was easy. As soon as Tina went back indoors, she greeted her mother with a hug and phoned a glazier to come and make Rose's back door safe.

'Lucky you were here,' Shirley said.

'No. Lucky Mel Blake had a parcel for her—I sometimes don't see Rose for a couple of days. I don't like to push too hard because I don't want her thinking I'm interfering or trying to take away her independence.' She sighed. 'If she's fractured a hip, it could take weeks— months—to heal. And then she'll need physio to help her to walk again. She'll need a fair bit of help at home, and it's not going to be easy to persuade her to accept any help.'

And this was just the excuse she needed to go and see Alex. To discuss a patient. 'Maybe I should pop down to the surgery and talk to Alex about her.'

The look Shirley gave her left Tina in no doubt that her mother saw straight through her, but that she was wise enough not to comment. 'You do that, love,' Shirley said.

Once Josh had challenged his grandmother to a game of Snakes and Ladders and was settled comfortably with a glass of milk and an apple, Tina walked down to Ellingthorpe Surgery. With any luck, she could catch Alex at the end of surgery. Talk to him about Rose…and then about their situation.

'I just need a quick word about a patient. I won't keep him long,' she said to Lorraine.

She was sitting leafing through a magazine when she

overheard a name she knew—a name that made the blood rush through her body.

'Dr A. Bowen.' The patient who'd spoken was reading down the list of staff on duty. 'Would that be Alex Bowen, by any chance?'

Trying not to look as though she was eavesdropping, Tina glanced over the edge of her magazine. The woman was standing in front of Lorraine, clearly arriving for an appointment or maybe to make one.

'Yes, that's right,' Lorraine confirmed.

Tina couldn't see the woman's face but guessed she was smiling. It showed in her voice.

'Alex Bowen. There couldn't be *two* doctors called Alex Bowen. Is he tall, dark and handsome with lovely eyes?'

'That's him.' Lorraine's answering smile broadened. 'And he's broken the heart of every woman around here, because he's completely unavailable.'

Unavailable? Tina's eyes widened in horror. Did everyone know what was happening between her and Alex? Or did Lorraine just mean what Maggie had told her, that Alex was known to be married to his work and all the single women in the village had given up trying to change his mind?

'Unavailable? He got married again, then? Oh, that's such good news. I knew him at his old practice, where I used to live, you see,' the woman explained. 'He's such a lovely man. It was a real tragedy.'

Tina's senses were on red alert. What tragedy? Alex had said something about a 'long story' and he hadn't wanted to discuss it at the time…but *tragedy*?

Luckily—or maybe unluckily—the patient was more than happy to tell Lorraine without any prompting. 'We were all so sorry when it happened—his poor little girl.'

Alex had a little girl? Since when? There wasn't a picture of her anywhere—not in his office, not in his home.
He'd never, ever mentioned a child to her, not even when
he'd been helping her to nurse Josh. Tina felt sick. There
had to be some mistake. Alex didn't have children.

'Only nine months old, she was. She'd have been
nearly seven now.'

She'd *died*?

But why hadn't Alex told her about it?

'I don't think any marriage could survive the loss of a
child,' the woman continued. 'You'll always blame yourself—or each other—and it can't have been more than six
months after that his wife left him. He left the village not
long after that. Poor, poor man. Still, if he's married again
and got another family, that's lovely.'

Alex *wasn't* married again, Tina thought sourly. And
as for the 'other family'… His little girl would have been
almost seven. Nearly two years older than Josh. Was that
why Alex had been attracted to her in the first place?
Because she came with a ready-made family, one very
like his own would have been?

A substitute.

Now it was clear why he'd never said he loved her.

Because he didn't.

He just wanted a child to replace the one he'd lost.

A wave of nausea engulfed her. She swallowed hard,
forcing it back. And when the patient sat down, busying
herself in a magazine, Tina went over to the reception
desk. 'Lorraine—sorry, I have to go.'

'Do you want me to give Alex a message?'

Tina shook her head. 'It doesn't matter now. I need to
get back to Josh. See you later.'

And as she walked back up the hill to her cottage, concentrating hard on holding back the tears, she thought her
heart would break.

CHAPTER THIRTEEN

To Tina's relief, her mother made no comment about how pale she looked or the tension in her face. She merely made Tina a sandwich, which Tina played with and crumbled on her plate. She couldn't eat anything right then—it would have choked her.

If only she hadn't gone to the surgery. If only she hadn't heard the truth about Alex's past.

Though maybe it was better she'd found out now, rather than committing herself to Alex and then discovering it was all an illusion. A *lie*.

When Shirley went home, Josh dragooned Tina into playing Snakes and Ladders with him, then beat her six times in a row. 'Mummy,' he said with a sigh and a shake of his head, 'you really have to pay attention. Look at people's faces when you play with them,' he added solemnly.

Exactly as she'd told him, countless times. Except she couldn't be amused this time at the way he'd quoted her. If she started laughing, she'd have cried.

'I'm sorry, darling. I've got something on my mind.'

'Nanny said Miss Larby had to go to hospital, like me. I saw the ambulance outside. The driver waved to me. Will Miss Larby get better?'

Rose. Tina flushed. She'd been so absorbed with the shocking news she'd heard about Alex, she hadn't even phoned to see how her neighbour was. 'I hope so, darling. I'll ring the hospital now and see how she's getting on.'

The receptionist at A and E put her through to the geriatric ward, where the nurse looking after Rose Larby told Tina that Rose had broken her hip. Tina sent Rose her love and the message that her window was fixed—the glazier had finished just before she'd returned home from the surgery—and promised to visit later.

'Miss Larby's going to be fine,' she told Josh. She poured him a glass of milk and gave him a banana. When he'd finished, she gave him a hug. 'And you need to have a rest.'

'I'm not tired, Mummy. And it's the middle of the day. I can't go to bed.'

'You weren't very well last week.' Understatement of the year. 'You really need to rest. Have a lie down—you can look at your rocks and minerals book if you like—and then we'll have another game of Snakes and Ladders and I'll beat you this time.'

Josh grinned. 'I'll beat *you*,' he retorted, and trotted upstairs.

Ten minutes later, he was asleep. Tina pottered around the house, unable to settle to anything—all she could think of was Alex, and how he'd lied to her.

When the doorbell rang, she knew exactly who it would be. She motioned him inside without comment, following him into the living room and choosing the furthest seat from his.

'Lorraine said you'd come to the surgery but left again, saying you needed to be back for Josh. Is everything all right?'

How could he sound so concerned, so worried about Josh, when he'd been lying to her all along?

'It's fine,' she said, but her voice sounded strained even to her own ears. 'I didn't come to see you about Josh. My neighbour, Rose Larby, had a fall and she's broken her hip. Though I didn't really need to bother you with it—I'll talk to the health visitor and Social Services myself. You had patients to see so I didn't wait.'

'Are you sure that's all? You look…' His voice faded as he took in the utter misery in her eyes.

'I'm fine,' she said through gritted teeth.

Of course she was fine. She'd just been saved from making the worst mistake of her life. And it hurt like hell. She wanted Alex—wanted him more than she'd wanted anyone, even Rod. She'd been prepared to put everything on the line for him, risk everything…and it had all been a lie. Because he hadn't trusted her. 'Why didn't you tell me, Alex?' she burst out.

'Tell you what?'

'About your little girl.'

He went white. 'How…?'

'It seems that one of your patients from your last practice has just moved into the village. She was chatting to Lorraine about you.'

'And Lorraine told you?'

She shook her head. 'She didn't need to—not that Lorraine would gossip, anyway. You know that.'

He flushed. 'Yes.'

'I was in the waiting room, so I heard every single word the patient said.' She folded her arms. 'You lied to me, Alex.'

A muscle worked in his jaw. 'I didn't.'

'Don't split hairs. A lie of omission is still a lie. You didn't tell me about your little girl—that she'd died. Don't you think I should have known about something as important as that?'

'And then what?' he demanded. 'You'd feel sorry for me? Or you'd think I wanted you—wanted *Josh*—as a substitute for the child I'd lost?'

The hit was dead on target. She flinched. 'That's what we are, though—aren't we? A substitute family.'

'Never.' He was emphatic.

'Then why didn't you tell me about your little girl?'

'Because…' He sighed. 'It's been six years, but it still hurts to talk about her.'

'And you think it doesn't hurt me to talk about Rod?' She shook her head. 'Alex, you knew I'd lost someone I loved. Didn't you think I'd understand?'

'I don't know what I thought,' he said helplessly. 'Tina…'

The sheer pain in his eyes made her want to run over to him, put her arms round him and promise she'd keep him safe. It was a physical wrench in her gut not to do it. But how could she ever trust him again? What other secrets was he keeping from her? And what secrets would he keep in the future? 'What else haven't you told me about?'

He reeled back as though she'd hit him. 'What do you want? My entire life story?'

'I don't want a relationship based on lies. But how can I trust you, when you've already kept something as big as this from me? When Jan lost her baby… It must have brought memories back for you.' Her voice cracked. 'You could have told me then. I wouldn't have pitied you—but I would have shared your grief. If you'd trusted me enough to share it.'

Alex was silent for a long, long time. For a moment, Tina actually thought he was going to get up and leave without explaining why he hadn't trusted her. And then he looked at her, his eyes dark with agony.

His little girl. How could he even begin to tell Tina about it? He hardly ever let himself think about his baby.

But if he didn't tell Tina everything, he'd lose her for ever.

'All right. If you want to know.' His voice was flat. 'I had a little girl, Bethany. She just didn't wake up one morning. She was nine months old when she died. The coroner said it was SIDS.'

SIDS, or sudden infant death syndrome, commonly known as cot death, was the leading cause of death for babies over a month old, killing around seven babies a week. Most babies who died were younger than six months, with a peak around the two-to-three-month mark, and it was more common in boys.

But the stats didn't even begin to reveal the heartache behind them, Alex thought savagely. How you walked into your baby's nursery, just to check she was sleeping peacefully—only to see an empty room, not even a cot, and the loss rushed over you once again when you re-membered she wasn't there any more. How you'd pack everything away, the tiny clothes and toys and books and pictures, and then suddenly you'd be looking in a drawer and come across a photograph and the loss would rip your heart apart again. Or someone who hadn't heard the news would ring and ask how the baby was doing. Or you'd be out somewhere and see a proud father pushing a pram and inside you'd be screaming to know *why* you didn't still have your baby to push round the park in a pram.

'I was away at a conference when it happened. My wife hadn't wanted me to go. But I went…' His voice cracked. 'And if I'd been at home, maybe I could have stopped Bethany dying.'

Tina shook her head. 'Of course you couldn't.'

'Isn't that how you felt about Rod? If you'd been there, you could have saved him? If you'd been there, Josh wouldn't have fallen from that slide and ended up with an extradural bleed?'

She gasped with shock. 'That's below the belt!'

'But it's true, isn't it? It's how you felt—it's how I felt, too. I'm a doctor. All those years of training—I should have been able to do something. I should have been able to save my daughter.'

'Not with cot death, Alex. You know there's no rhyme or reason for it.'

Although many SIDS babies were found dead in their cots, it could happen at any time of day, not just night. And although premature and low-birthweight babies were more at risk, any baby could be affected. The cause of death was always unexplained.

'We did all the right things,' Alex said. He stared into the distance, seeing his daughter's face in his mind's eye. The chubby little fingers that had waved excitedly to him; the fine, fluffy hair that had started to form dark ringlets; the little arms that had flopped back to lie beside her head while she'd slept; the gummy smile that had revealed four tiny white teeth; the dark eyes that had sparkled with love and joy; her rich, deep chuckle when he'd played a bouncing game with her. He could almost smell that soft baby smell, a mixture of baby lotion and milk, and a tremor ran through him.

'We put her in the feet-to-foot position in her cot, didn't let her get too hot, kept her cot in our room for the first six months, wouldn't let anyone smoke within a mile of her. But...' he closed his eyes briefly '...she still died. Vivi—my wife—went into her room that morning, and Bethany just wouldn't wake up.'

His voice was hoarse with strain; he could feel tears stinging the back of his eyes and he willed them back.

He wasn't going to cry. Not now. He'd hit the depths six years ago and he'd cried himself out then.

And Tina wanted to know why he couldn't trust? He took a deep breath. 'Vivi thought it was my fault, too. If I hadn't gone away, if I'd been there, Bethany wouldn't have died. Vivi built a wall between us, and I didn't have a clue how to get through it, how to comfort her.' A bitter smile twisted his face. 'Though other men didn't have quite the same problem. My best friend in particular.'

Tina's eyes widened, appalled. 'You mean...?'

He nodded. 'I came home early from surgery one day. Neither of them was expecting me. They were making love in *our* bed.' He could still remember it. It had seemed to happen in slow motion, like a film. He'd come home and the house had been silent. Vivi's car had been outside so he'd thought she'd been asleep. He'd walked upstairs quietly so he didn't wake her, then had heard his wife crying out. A cry he recognised as passion, not fear. His first thought had been disbelief, then denial. He'd pushed the door open, the sound of his pulse booming in his ears, and seen them there. The two people he'd loved and trusted most in the world. Betraying him.

He swallowed hard. 'Vivi walked out on me that afternoon to go with him. I couldn't stand being the object of pity in the village, so I left. I came here, where nobody knew me, where nobody could think of me as ''poor Alex'', and I swore I'd never, ever get involved with another woman again. I threw myself into my work and that was fine.'

Until he'd met Tina. She'd somehow brushed all the hurt away, made him want to trust again. Except he hadn't been able to tell her. Until now, when it was too late.

'So. Now you know.'

'I'm sorry, Alex.'

He shook his head. 'Doesn't matter now. It was my fault anyway.'

'How do you make that out?' she demanded.

'I was hopeless at relationships. I always have been—right from the word go,' he said. 'I wasn't a lovable child. I can't blame my parents for wanting to spend more time at work than with me. The nannies never stayed that long either.' He sighed. 'I loved Bethany—I would have laid down my life for my daughter. But she was so little when she died. I never had the chance to really know her, like the way you know Josh. Maybe if I had… Well, I was no good as a son or a husband. I wouldn't have been a good father either.' He swallowed. 'The first time I saw you, you were hopping up the hill with Josh, the pair of you laughing, with purple hair. I thought then, I couldn't imagine my mother ever doing that. She never took me to school. It was always the nanny's job.'

And now his worst fears had come true. Those violet-blue eyes were filled with pity. Any moment now she was going to hold him. But not because she *wanted* him—because she felt sorry for him. He lifted his chin, his eyes flashing a warning at her to keep her distance.

'I wanted her to love me, but then I became a GP. She never forgave me for it.'

Tina frowned. 'But—weren't your parents *proud* you became a doctor?'

He smiled mirthlessly. 'I don't think you understand. My father is Anthony Bowen.'

'The neurologist?' Tina could remember making notes as a student from a textbook by Anthony Bowen. Alex's father was *famous*.

He nodded. 'And my mother is Amanda Bowen.'

'The oncology professor?' Tina had seen Amanda Bowen's name on countless conference papers. If anything, she was even more well-known than her husband. Alex had had a lot to live up to.

'Amanda thought I'd follow in her footsteps—or, if not hers, my father's. But I didn't want a career where I never knew whether I'd earned my position fairly or it had been given to me because of who my parents were. Either that, or I'd have to work twice as hard as anyone else to prove that I was capable of doing the job and it wasn't just nepotism. Besides, I didn't want to spend my life stuck in a lab or in some research faculty. I wanted to work with people.' He smiled mirthlessly. 'Funny that, the first time I tried to do something to please Amanda—spoke at a conference—my whole life crashed into dust.'

'She must have been upset about what happened—about losing Bethany.'

Alex shrugged. 'She sent flowers. But she'd never approved of Vivi. She couldn't understand how I could possibly want to marry a practice receptionist when there were all those clever, pretty girls at med school.'

Tina knew exactly how Alex's wife must have felt. Amanda Bowen sounded as if she had a lot in common with the Turnbulls, planning her son's future and refusing to recognise anything that got in their way.

'She's dead now. Funny how a world-renowned oncology expert can ignore the signs of cancer in herself. How she can leave a curable form of the disease until it was too late and she'd developed mets.' Mets—properly known as metastases—or secondary cancers developed if the primary tumour was left untreated; they in turn would spread until there was nothing the doctors could do except offer palliative care to relieve pain.

He spoke lightly, but Tina could sense the depth of pain beneath his words. 'Alex…'

'Now you know everything. I let my parents down, I let my wife down, I let my baby down.'

'No, you didn't.' This time Tina ignored the warning flash in his eyes and crossed over to his chair, sitting on the arm and taking his hand in hers. 'It's not your fault, Alex. None of it was.'

'No? I think I fell in love with Vivi because she was the opposite of my mother. She was always laughing, affectionate and fun to be with. I loved her and I thought she'd love me, too, but I wanted too much from her.' He disentangled his hand from hers. 'And I've done the same with you.'

Fallen in love with her? Seen her as the opposite of his mother? Or wanted too much from her?

She sighed. 'I just wish you'd trusted me earlier.'

'And told you what? That I was an emotional mess, I'd been an unlovable child and a useless husband?'

'That's not true, Alex. You weren't unlovable—maybe your parents were just wrapped up in their work. Have you ever thought that *they* might have been the ones at fault?'

'Once,' he admitted. 'But then I failed again with Vivi.'

'Sometimes marriage is like that. People change, grow apart. How old were you when you met Vivi?'

'Twenty-six.'

'And she was?'

'Twenty-one.'

'Exactly. You were both young.' She and Rod had met at nineteen—but they'd been lucky and had grown together rather than in different directions. 'Maybe you just met at the wrong time. And you can't blame yourself for Bethany's death.'

He ignored her. 'You were already hurting. Would you have listened if I'd told you I loved you?'

She was silent. *Would* she have listened?

He sighed. 'I thought not. When Josh asked you if I'd be his new daddy, you threw me out.'

'You're not the only one who's made mistakes,' she said quietly. 'I needed time to think it through. There's not just me to consider in a relationship any more—there's Josh. If everything goes wrong, his world gets shattered, as well as mine. I can't take risks.'

'And I thought I was supposed to be the one with a trust problem,' Alex said. His tone was light, but Tina could see the pain in his eyes.

'I'm sorry. But...you didn't tell me. And when I heard what that woman said, I thought...I thought you wanted Josh as a substitute.'

Alex shook his head. 'I loved him for his own sake.'

Tina noted the past tense. *Loved.* Did that mean Alex had changed his mind? And what about her? Did he love her? Tina didn't dare ask. She wasn't sure what the answer was and she didn't want to hear the wrong one. 'I'm sorry, Alex. I...' She sighed. 'I don't know what to say.'

'That makes two of us.' He paused. 'So where do we go now?'

She shook her head. 'I don't know.' She bit her lip. 'I told you, my neighbour had a fall. While we were waiting for the ambulance, she told me about the man she'd wanted to marry but her family didn't like him. She said he'd died in the war and she always wished she'd taken the risk.' There was a long, long silence. 'That was what I came to tell you today.'

'And then you heard Mrs Yeats talking about Bethany. And changed your mind.'

'It was the fact you hadn't told me. That you'd kept secrets.' She bit her lip. 'Though maybe I'm not being fair. I more or less poured out my whole life story to you. I shouldn't expect you to do the same.'

'Or maybe you should. What use is love without trust?'

And that was the whole point. *Could* she trust Alex again?

The imp on Alex's shoulder shrugged. *You've already blown it. Why don't you tell her the rest?*

No point. She wouldn't want to hear it.

Tell her anyway. You've got nothing left to lose.

'I love you.'

'What?' Tina stared at him in disbelief.

'It's crazy. I know. You're not ready for another relationship, I've made a mess of every relationship I've ever had, and…I love you,' he said simply.

And the rest, the imp prodded.

'I was going to ask you to marry me.'

'Marry you?' she echoed.

'Grow old with me. Give Josh a brother and a sister. Share the love—and the worry. A true partnership. I'd love Josh as my own and I'd never see him as second to our other children.' He shrugged. 'But you're right. Without trust, there's no point. So just forget I said anything.'

She stared at him without saying a word.

He stood up. 'I'd better go. I'm sorry, Tina. I really wanted things to be different.' He dug his nails into his palms to keep his control in place. 'I'll stay out of your way as much as possible at work, so don't hand your notice in—the practice needs you.' He forced a smile to his face. 'I'll see myself out.'

'No.' She stood up and placed her hand on his arm. 'Alex—I don't know what to say. I've coped on my own with Josh since Rod died. Except when he had the accident and you were there for me. And I really, really appreciated it.'

'But I'm not what you want.' His mouth tightened. 'Spare me the pity, Tina. I've had enough pity to last me a lifetime.'

'It's not pity.' There were tears in her eyes now, but he couldn't tell if they were tears of pain or anger. 'I just need time to sort my head out, Alex. To work out how I feel—to untangle all the guilt and the longing and the fear and everything else.'

Guilt—that was Rod. Fear—he knew all about that. Longing? A tiny flicker of hope sprang up in his heart. And hadn't she said she'd come to the surgery to tell him she wanted to take the risk?

Maybe—just maybe—this was going to work out.

'I just need time,' she said again. 'Maybe if we stay out of each other's way for a week—we don't see each other, we don't talk on the phone—maybe we just need space to work out how we feel.'

'A week?'

'A week,' she confirmed.

Seven days. One hundred and sixty-eight hours. Over ten thousand minutes. This was going to take his self-endurance way beyond anything that had tested him in the past. But if that was what it took... 'Call me when you're ready,' he said. And left before he pulled her into his arms and begged her never to leave him.

CHAPTER FOURTEEN

WITHIN a day Tina was miserable. But she'd said a week. A week. A whole week without Alex. She must have been crazy.

I love you... Grow old with me...

She wanted to. How she wanted to.

Yet there was still the question of trust.

She could understand now why Alex hadn't told her about Bethany. He was convinced he was unlovable. With parents who had been more concerned with their work than their son, and a wife who'd betrayed him with his best friend, that was hardly surprising. He was scared to love again.

And she was equally scared—she had so much to lose if it all went wrong.

But if she didn't take the risk...would she spend the rest of her life regretting it, like Rose Larby had?

She had a second chance to make things work.

But it had to be right. For both of them.

Alex threw himself into work. When he wasn't seeing patients, he made inroads into his backlog of paperwork and administrative tasks. He took on extra duties, swapped shifts with others at the practice and made sure that every single second of his time was busy. Because when it wasn't, he thought of Tina. And longed for her.

On the second day without Alex, Tina developed insomnia. She sat on the kitchen doorstep, looking up at the stars. The same stars that Alex might be watching even now. The thought comforted her.

On the third day, she'd had enough. She picked up the phone and rang him.

'Hello, this is Alex. I can't come to the phone right now, so leave your name and number after the long tone and I'll call you back.'

She cut the connection before the answering-machine beeped at her. This wasn't a message she wanted to leave on an answering-machine. It was pointless ringing now anyway. He was probably still at the surgery—his list might be running late, or maybe he'd had to slot in an emergency.

She'd dialled the first four numbers of the surgery before she realised what she was doing.

Leave it, she told herself. Ring him at lunchtime.

But his answering-machine was still on then.

She rang again at three, only to hear the recorded message again. Then she had the brainwave of trying his mobile.

'The phone you are calling is switched off,' a voice informed her. 'Please, try later.'

Alex was a GP. He almost never switched his mobile off—not unless he was in a hospital, near equipment that could be affected by a mobile phone. Tina started to get worried. Where was he? This time she dialled the surgery's full number.

'Good afternoon, Ellingthorpe Surgery.'

'Lorraine, it's Tina. Is…um… Is Alex around?'

'No. He's off this afternoon—though I think he said something about having to make a house call. Can anyone else help?'

'Thanks, but no. I'll try him later.'

'Try his mobile,' Lorraine suggested.

Tina almost told her she'd already done it, but stopped herself just in time. Alex didn't need any more gossip about him in the practice. Although Lorraine was discreet, what Mrs Yeats had told her would have worried her enough to tell the other partners and Maggie, the practice manager. Alex had probably had three days of hell and maybe that was why he'd switched his mobile off. To get some peace. 'Cheers, Lorraine,' she said, and hung up.

'Thank goodness you've come, Dr Bowen,' Ellen Barker said. 'I didn't know who else to call. I thought the police…but then that might tip Jim over the edge.' She wrung her hands together. 'He's still locked in the barn. Whenever I try to talk to him, he just tells me to go away and forget all about him. I'm so scared he's going to do something stupid. He's…' Her voice shook. 'I think he's got a shotgun with him.'

'I can't promise I'll be able to help him, but I'll do my best,' Alex reassured her. Though his heart sank. Jim was in the most at-risk group of potential suicides, being male, older and with his business in difficulties. Would the support of his family be enough to stop him trying to end it all?

'I wanted him to come and see you before,' Ellen said as she led Alex to the barn, 'though he kept telling me not to be so daft, there was nothing wrong with him. But he's been that down. He hasn't slept properly for months and half the time he feeds his dinner to the dog, thinking I don't know what he's doing. It was his great-grandfather's farm and he thinks he's let the whole family down.' Her lips thinned. 'It's not his fault we got swine fever last year. We weren't the only ones. Why can't he see that?'

Classic symptoms of depression, Alex thought. Problems sleeping, loss of appetite, feelings of worthlessness and guilt. 'It's been tough this year, too?' he guessed.

She nodded. 'He found out this morning the sugar beet crop's been infected with a virus—it's practically worthless now. And he just snapped—he walked out of the office. He wouldn't even let the dog go with him, though she ran after him. She's been sitting right outside the barn door ever since and she won't leave—will you, girl?' She fondled the ears of the black Labrador. 'Let's hope Dr Bowen can talk some sense into him, Suki.'

Alex rapped on the door. 'Mr Barker?'

There was no answer. His gut tightened. But Jim Barker couldn't have shot himself—his wife would have heard the gunshot. 'Mr Barker,' he tried again, 'it's Alex Bowen. Can I have a quick word with you, please?'

That got a response. 'No. I don't need you and your sort. Leave me be.'

'Mr Barker—your wife's worried sick about you. So's the dog. Just let me talk to you for a moment.'

'They're better off without me. All of them,' Jim called back.

'They don't think so. And neither do I.'

'Go away and leave me alone.'

'It might make you feel better if you talk to me,' Alex said.

'You?' There was a derisive laugh. 'You live in one of those fancy barn conversions. You and your money—you don't have a clue what it's like.'

'To face tough times financially, no,' Alex said. 'But I lost something much more valuable. Something money couldn't buy. At the time, it felt as if my world ended and there was no point in going on. I've come out the other side, though it took me a long while.'

Silence. Alex only hoped that his words had go

through—that he'd reassured Jim that depression could hit anyone at any time, and there was no stigma attached to it.

'Mr Barker, I'm going to ask your wife to bring us a flask of tea,' Alex said, looking enquiringly at Ellen, who nodded and headed back to the farmhouse. 'Will you let me in while she's gone?'

'What did you lose?' Jim Barker demanded suddenly.

'My baby daughter,' Alex said. 'She died.'

There was a long, long pause. And then Alex heard a scraping sound as Jim pulled back the bolt.

'Thank you,' Alex said quietly.

'You're not going to change my mind,' Jim stated, still holding the gun.

'You're planning to use that gun on yourself?'

'What if I am?'

'Will you talk to me first?'

'Not much point in talking, is there? Not when I'm going to have the bailiffs in to take away everything. Over a hundred years my family's had this farm. Over a hundred years. And I've lost it.'

Alex knew the value of silence and just let Jim talk.

'Last year, with the pigs—it was bad. But we got compensation.' He laughed bitterly. 'Nowhere near enough, mind, and it'd take years to build my herd back up to what it was. And then I decided to switch from barley to sugar beet. Worst thing I've ever done—the land's got rhizomania. You know what that is, Dr Bowen?'

'Mad sugar beet disease?' Alex guessed.

'That's what the papers call it. It's a virus. Sucks the sugar out of the roots so they're not worth as much—and you lose tonnage, too, because the roots are all thin and beardlike instead of fat and juicy. The lower field had a couple of boggy patches in it and I didn't like the look of the plants. There were clumps of them in the field with lots of small yellow leaves—I thought maybe they just needed a bit of nitrogen, but sent them off for testing anyway. And they rang me this morning to tell me what it was. Rhizomania. It stays in the soil for fifteen years, so there's an end to my beet crops.'

'Aren't there some virus-resistant varieties of beet?' Alex asked.

'Yes, but they're no good to me, are they? They have to be tested before you know whether they'll work in your soil—that costs money and time, and all my money's invested in the crop out there. I might just as well have taken the money out of the bank and burned it.' Jim shook his head. 'There's no hope. And what are you going to give me? Happy pills? Something to dope me up and keep me quiet?'

'No. Though I might be able to give you something that'll help you sleep and give you your appetite back—and that'll go some way to helping you feel well enough to tackle what's worrying you.'

Jim gave a short laugh. 'I wouldn't even know where to start.'

'The farm's gone through lean times before, hasn't it?'

He shrugged. 'I suppose so.'

'And you came through it before.'

'That was then.' Jim snorted in disgust. 'I might as well sell off the land to a developer and let them build houses.'

'That's one solution,' Alex said.

'One.' Jim scowled. 'I don't know why I bother anyway. The kids don't want to work on the land—there isn't enough money in it for them. I might as well give it all up now.'

'What would you do if you weren't a farmer?'

Jim shrugged. 'Dunno. A farmer's all I ever wanted to

be. Like my dad and my grandad and my great-grandad.'
He looked at Alex. 'Didn't you always want to be a doctor?'

'Until my little girl died, yes. Then I thought about giving it all up—I'd been no use to her,' Alex said.

'But you're still a doctor.'

Alex nodded. 'The day I was going to chuck it all in, I went for a long walk by the river. Some of the village kids had been playing by the weir and one of them fell in—I told the others to call an ambulance and managed to get her out. The girl's mother came round later and told me I'd saved her life. If I hadn't been a doctor, hadn't known what to do to resuscitate her, she'd have died.' He shrugged. 'So then I thought about it. All that training—it was stupid to waste it.'

'It's different for me. I'm a dead loss. Who wants a farmer? What use am I to anyone?'

'I think your family could answer that better than I can,' Alex said. 'Your wife loves you. What would she do without you?'

'She'd get over it.'

'Are you sure about that?' Alex asked, thinking of Tina. He didn't think he'd ever get over her if he lost her. 'And your dog. She'd pine away. What about your kids? Are you going to teach them that the way to cope with your problems is to kill yourself?'

Jim swung the gun round and pointed it at Alex. 'Are you telling me I'm a coward?'

The back of Alex's neck prickled. Jim was angry, hurt, frightened—desperate. Would he really pull the trigger? And who would he aim the gun at when he did it?

Please, no, he thought. I want to live. I need to see Tina. Tell her how much I love her. Make her see it's worth taking a chance.

He took a deep breath, aware that his hands were shaking and hoping that his voice didn't betray the fear he felt. 'No. I'm just telling you to think about what you're doing. You've had a run of bad luck—worse than most—but you're a fighter, Jim, not a quitter. If you kill yourself, what's Ellen going to do? How's she going to stand living around here, knowing you killed yourself? How's she going to cope without you? She's right by your side, Jim. She loves you. Are you going to tell her that love's worth nothing?'

Jim didn't answer, but he lowered the gun's muzzle.

'This is a good place to live and work, Jim,' Alex said quietly. 'You've got plenty of people round here who support you—who respect you. It's not going to be easy, but you'll get through this. You've got your family and friends behind you. And all of us need help from time to time—don't be too proud to accept it.'

'I'm still not taking happy pills.'

'I'm not going to force you to take anything,' Alex said. 'But depression's a real illness and it has real symptoms. You can't sleep, you can't eat, you can't concentrate, your hands are sweating—I can help you with all that so you don't have to cope with them as well as your business.'

'Depression,' Jim sneered. 'It's just people swinging the lead.'

'It's ordinary people like you and me,' Alex said. 'And you'd be surprised how many need a little bit of help. It's nothing to be ashamed of. And nobody needs to know about it except you and me.' He paused, then said quietly, 'Give me the gun, Jim. Please.'

Jim said nothing. Time stretched as Alex waited. And waited. And waited.

And finally Jim nodded and handed over the gun.

'Thank you,' Alex said. 'I promise you, you won't regret this. Give the antidepressants a try. I'll write you a prescription and I want you to start taking them tonight, before bed. They'll take three or four weeks to start working, but you should find they help. And I want you to come and see me in surgery tomorrow.' If he told Jim why, the farmer was obstinate enough to refuse—but in the morning, Jim would hopefully be in a more receptive state of mind when Alex suggested a course of counselling.

Jim coughed. 'Dr Bowen—that business about the gun… Are you going to the police?'

Alex shook his head. 'Though until you're feeling better, I'll advise Ellen to keep the keys to your gun cabinet and not to let you have them.' He smiled. 'If anything, you did me a favour.'

'How do you make that out, then?'

'Because when I thought you were going to shoot me, it made me realise there's something I really, really have to do.' Something he had to say. Something that couldn't wait another four days. At Jim's puzzled frown, Alex added, 'This is just between you and me…but I hope you're going to be dancing at my wedding.'

'Dancing?'

'Dancing,' Alex confirmed.

When Alex left the Barkers' farm, he drove straight home. He'd just picked up the phone when his doorbell rang.

His eyes widened when he opened the door. 'Tina. I was just going to…' His voice faded. No. Please. She can't have decided so soon—decided it's not going to work. Please.

'Can I come in?' she asked.

'Of course. Where's Josh?'

'With my parents. Making spaceship biscuits, I think.'

'Tina—'

'Alex—'

They both spoke at the same time, and stopped. 'You first,' Tina said.

Tell her, the imp demanded.

'This afternoon, something happened that made me realise how I really feel about you. I thought about what life would be like without you—and I couldn't bear it. And I couldn't wait another four days. I was going to phone you to tell you again that I love you and I want you for ever. That goes for Josh, too.' He paused. 'Now you.'

'You've said it all for me,' she said quietly. 'I've been thinking, too. These past three days without you…they've been miserable. I love you, I want to spend the rest of my life with you—and I want the rest of my life to start right now.'

He pulled her into his arms and kissed her. Thoroughly.

'So you'll marry me, then?' he asked when he broke the kiss.

'How can you ask me when I can't think straight enough to answer?' she grumbled.

'One little word,' he coaxed. 'Yes or no?'

Tina paused. 'Rod…what we had…'

'Was special,' Alex supplied. 'You and me—it doesn't change the past. Rod will always be part of your life, through Josh, and you'll always love him. I respect that.' He brushed her lower lip with his thumb. 'But now it's time to move on—for both of us.'

'Together,' she added.

'So are you going to marry me, Tina Lawson? To have and to hold, for the rest of our lives?'

She smiled. 'What do you think?'

'I need to hear you say it.'

She stopped teasing him. 'Yes.'

EPILOGUE

Ten months later…

'WHAT do you think?' Alex asked.

Josh stood back and eyed him critically. 'You need a bit more.'

'I'm in your hands, son,' he said with a grin.

Josh set to work with the spray, and finally nodded in satisfaction. 'Cool. What about me?'

Alex surveyed him for a moment. 'Cool. Come on, let's go and show your mum.'

Josh raced up the stairs and rapped on his mother's bedroom door. Alex followed at a more sedate pace, carrying a tray of tea and toast.

'Mummy, we've brought you some breakfast,' Josh called.

'Come in,' Tina called back.

When the door opened, her chin nearly hit the floor. 'Purple hair. You've both got…purple hair!' she gurgled.

'Now, let me see. How does it go? ''I'm doing a fundraiser for my son's school. They're having a mad hair day. Anyone who comments about my hair can give some money to school funds. Starting with you.''' Alex smiled sweetly at his wife and rattled a tin at her.

'You're not *seriously* going to work like that.'

'You did,' he pointed out, laughing.

'Yes, but—'

'And, unlike some people,' he said, batting his eyelashes at her, 'I checked it'd wash out first.'

'You can do it with us next year, Mummy,' Josh informed her kindly. 'We can spray the baby's hair purple as well.'

'You'll do no such thing, Joshua Bowen,' Tina said tartly, sitting up and adjusting her bump.

'But the baby'll have hair. She'll be eleven months old then,' Josh said. 'Won't she, Daddy?'

'The baby might be a boy,' Alex reminded him, ruffling his hair and then looking with dismay at the purple stain on his hand.

'Serves you right,' Tina said, sticking her tongue out.

Alex grinned. 'You're only jealous because you're not up to waddling up the hill with us.'

'Huh.' Tina pulled a face at him. 'More like you wouldn't let me.'

'And what would you say to any of your patients who wanted to hop up the hill at eight months pregnant?' Alex asked sweetly.

'Oh, stop fussing.' Tina ate a bite of her toast. 'Did you put any Marmite on this?'

'Tons,' Josh said. 'Your tastebuds are just funny. Come on, Daddy. We're going to be late if we don't go now.'

Alex rolled his eyes. 'OK, OK, son, I'm coming.'

Son. He still couldn't quite believe how quickly Josh had accepted him in his life. The first question Josh had asked, when they'd broken the news of their wedding to him, had been, 'Will you be my daddy?' His second had been, 'Now can we have a dog?' And the third, Alex thought with an inward grin, had been, 'Can I have a baby sister?'

Alex bent down to kiss his wife. 'I'll see you later. And remember you're supposed to be resting—which doesn't mean cleaning out the kitchen cupboards or hanging curtains or doing a pile of ironing.' He stole another kiss, and placed another on the bump, which promptly kicked him.

'I love you, Tina Bowen.' His smile broadened. 'You, and our son, and The Bump. Our family.'

'Our family,' she echoed, lifting her mug of tea in a toast.

Modern Romance™
...seduction and
passion guaranteed

Tender Romance™
...love affairs that
last a lifetime

Medical Romance™
...medical drama
on the pulse

Historical Romance™
...rich, vivid and
passionate

Sensual Romance™
...sassy, sexy and
seductive

Blaze Romance™
...the temperature's
rising

27 new titles every month.

Live the emotion

MILLS & BOON®

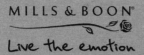

Medical Romance™

THE PREGNANCY PROPOSITION
by Meredith Webber

Nurse Amelia Peterson's relationship with A&E
consultant 'Mac' McDougal had always been rocky.
She was astonished when he asked her out one night
...and even more surprised when she woke up with
him the next morning! Mac doesn't do relationships,
but he had always wanted a child. And then Amelia
realised she was pregnant...

A WHITE KNIGHT IN ER *by Jessica Matthews*

ER nurse Megan Erickson needs all the support she can
get after a broken engagement and becoming mother
to her brother's young children. The attention of ER
physician Jonas Taylor, with his playboy reputation, is
the last thing she needs. But when an accident in ER
has serious implications for Megan, Jonas reveals
himself as her knight in shining armour!

THE SURGEON'S CHILD *by Alison Roberts*

Consultant surgeon Matt Saunders suffered when his
child's existence was kept from him, but his intimate
relationship with paediatric nurse Polly Martin is the
start of a passionate relationship. Soon Polly has a
secret of her own – she's pregnant. Her news might
push Matt away – but if she doesn't tell him, then
surely he'll feel betrayed all over again?

On sale 1st August 2003

*Available at most branches of WH Smith, Tesco, Martins, Borders,
Eason, Sainsbury's and all good paperback bookshops.*

0703/03a

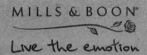

MILLS & BOON®

Live the emotion

Medical Romance™

DR MARCO'S BRIDE *by Carol Wood*

Dr Marco Dallori has come to England for six months. He isn't looking for love – he's got a young son to consider, as well as his own bruised heart. Dr Kelly Anders can't help being attracted to Marco – his Latin looks are irresistible. But she knows a temporary affair is all she can hope for. Unless she can convince this Italian doctor that he needs a bride...

MEDITERRANEAN RESCUE *by Laura MacDonald*

Nurse Claire Schofield was on holiday in Rome when an earthquake threw her together with Dr Dominic Hansford. Working side by side led to one unforgettable night of pleasure, and Claire returned home with her heart full of her secret lover. But at the hospital where she now works a new locum has been appointed, and his dark good looks are *very* familiar...

THE BABY SPECIALIST *by Rebecca Lang*

When theatre nurse Leila Hardwick discovers that the new obs and gynae surgeon is Dr Rupert Daniels she tries to keep her identity secret. Her sister once tried to seduce him into having a baby. But Leila cannot escape Rupert's allure, and eventually he discovers who she is. Rupert seems as tempted by Leila as she is by him – but he avoids emotional commitment at all costs...

On sale 1st August 2003

Available at most branches of WH Smith, Tesco, Martins, Borders, Eason, Sainsbury's and all good paperback bookshops.

0703/03b

Don't miss *Book Twelve* of this BRAND-NEW 12 book collection 'Bachelor Auction'.

Who says money can't buy love?

On sale 1st August

4 FREE

books and a surprise gift!

We would like to take this opportunity to thank you for reading this Mills & Boon® book by offering you the chance to take FOUR more specially selected titles from the Medical Romance™ series absolutely FREE! We're also making this offer to introduce you to the benefits of the Reader Service™—

- ★ FREE home delivery
- ★ FREE gifts and competitions
- ★ FREE monthly Newsletter
- ★ Exclusive Reader Service discount
- ★ Books available before they're in the shops

Accepting these FREE books and gift places you under no obligation to buy, you may cancel at any time, even after receiving your free shipment. Simply complete your details below and return the entire page to the address below. *You don't even need a stamp!*

YES! Please send me 4 free Medical Romance books and a surprise gift. I understand that unless you hear from me, I will receive 6 superb new titles every month for just £2.60 each, postage and packing free. I am under no obligation to purchase any books and may cancel my subscription at any time. The free books and gift will be mine to keep in any case.

M3ZEE

Ms/Mrs/Miss/Mr ....Initials................................
                                          BLOCK CAPITALS PLEASE
Surname ....

Address ....

....

....Postcode...................................

Send this whole page to:
UK: FREEPOST CN81, Croydon, CR9 3WZ
EIRE: PO Box 4546, Kilcock, County Kildare (stamp required)